DIVINE SARAH

ALSO BY ADAM BRAVER

Mr. Lincoln's Wars

DIVINE SARAH

ADAM BRAVER

wm WILLIAM MORROW *An Imprint of* HarperCollins*Publishers*

Photograph of Sarah Bernhardt in the role of Junie in *Britannicus*
c. 1860 by Gaspard Felix Tournachon Nadar courtesy of the
Musée de la Ville de Paris, Musée Carnavalet, Paris, France/
Archives Charmet/Bridgeman Art Library.

HarperCollins books may be purchased for educational,
business, or sales promotional use. For information please
write: Special Markets Department, HarperCollins Publishers
Inc., 10 East 53rd Street, New York, NY 10022.

FIRST EDITION

Designed by Shubhani Sarkar

Printed on acid-free paper

Library of Congress Cataloging-in-Publication Data

Braver, Adam, 1963–
    Divine Sarah / Adam Braver.—1st ed.
      p. cm.
    ISBN 0-06-054407-4 (acid-free paper)
    1. Bernhardt, Sarah, 1844–1923—Fiction.   2. Actresses—
Fiction. 3. France—Fiction. I. Title.

PS3602.R39D57   2004
813'.6—dc22

                             2003062395

04 05 06 07 08 ✤/RRD 10 9 8 7 6 5 4 3 2 1

24

FOR ALISSON AND ADDISON

I would rather go to the theater and feast my eyes on the scenery, in which I find my dearest dreams artistically expressed and tragically concentrated. These things, because they are false, are infinitely closer to the truth.

CHARLES BAUDELAIRE

American Debut, Performance No. 27
Booth Theater, New York City

SHE has paced the boards for nearly three hours. Twirling and jumping and falling. She hasn't even noticed her dresses weighted down by Lepaul's embroidered pearls and roses. She has been Marguerite Gautier in *La Dame aux Camélias* for five acts, portraying a moment-by-moment life in tragic pursuit of Armand Duval.

Feet gliding effortlessly.

Wincing and smiling while changing partners.

Moving in delight along the freedom of the stage.

Absorbing the lines of the script.

Smelling the Parisian air.

Ingesting the calm of Bougival.

Clutching the bitter eyes of those who betray her.

Embracing the eyes of those who will love her.

Tasting the pain of regret and longing.

Higher than morphine, opium, and hashish all ingested together.

And now it is the final scene. A mid-afternoon light breaks through the window. In her bed. Her entire body convulses and she sits upward, then melts and slumps against the mattress. Cells ravaged by tuberculosis while her heart pounds with its first true honest emotion—fear. And the breath slips out of her chest, rising and falling in rapid rhythm. She tries to capture each exhalation. Hold on to it. Confine it into her memory as though her brain can be a repository, a subterfuge that cheats the lungs of their intended malfeasance. On her upper lip is a smudge of red theater paint to simulate the last exit of blood that has trailed through her nose. As she lies on the damp sheets, the weight of dying having shoved her from her body, she grips down for the floorboards, clawing at each plank with the secret hope that one will break from its nails and allow her to crawl away into a world where the murder of disease cannot find her. Her eyes are barely open. She swears she sees blood drop down the sheets and onto the floor. Her own blood, falling and betraying her. Then she grasps one more time at the floor, her last measure of strength to escape consumption's embrace. And there in her bed she dies. Leaving her eyes partway open, because the dead really only close their eyes under the physician's hand.

And a curtain drops.

The steady rattle of applause. The tentative clapping from the front, not wholly positive about the appropriateness of their timing, and not quite willing to concede the mood and return to the necessities of finding coat-check tickets, deciding which exit to take, and which social fraternities to avoid.

But soon it spreads. Is it a thunderstorm? The crashing of

waves? A pounding white noise fills the theater until it is no longer a sound, but the norm of silence.

Behind the curtain she has difficulty lifting herself up. The vestiges of disease still debilitate her. She wipes the back of her hand against her nose. It is dry. No trace of blood. Just a thick oil paint. She should hold a hand for balance but is not quite ready for human contact. Her eyes are still partway closed. She is not fully of this world yet.

The curtain rises, and through the lighting of the footlights she sees the ghostly outline of the front-row patrons rolling back and multiplying into the balconies. They are all on their feet. Eyes focused on her. Every ounce of energy that wills them to life is directed to her, a thousand beams of force funneled and aimed. Love. Adoration. Thankfulness. It rocks the walls. Swings the chandeliers. Artificially pumps her heart.

Twenty-eight more times the curtain rises and falls. Each time the clapping and cheering sound as loud as they can get. Then she steps back onto the stage, and there is another surge, rising the volume to a new level. She bows. She tries to reach out a hand to every member of the audience, mouthing *merci*, her eyes glistening, genuinely touched, her body weakened from having battled dying and the subsequent reincarnation.

After the twenty-ninth curtain call she instructs the promoter, a man named Jarrett, to turn on the houselights. She collapses on the backstage couch. Her entire being racked by exhaustion. Max Klein, her manager, is there. Her sister is there also. The road through America has been one grand circus of an adventure. But tonight she is fatigued. The soul of Marguerite Gautier has stripped her bare. There will be no parties. No nightclubs. No drugs. No sex. She will just go back to the Albemarle Hotel and collapse into her bed. Let the dying take her into a slumber that leaves her void of the workings of the heart and mind for the next eight hours.

But then Jarrett tells her that there are at least five thousand people waiting at the theater door. Many have been there since she first entered. Trying to cut her hair from under her feathered hat. Pinning broaches on her. Handing off bouquets. Begging for signatures. In books. On cuffs. On forearms. And all those hands had tried to touch her. No real purpose, no assigned motive other than the possibility of wanting to connect, to feel adoration. And she was gracious. She might have stayed longer if the scissors had not aimed for her hair, whence the security guard grabbed her to be ushered into the safety of the Booth. Now the crowd has multiplied. She is no longer just the center of Paris, and then Europe. She is now the center of New York City. She is conquering America. The world. They all want her presence. As if her presence is somehow a sign of hope.

She is tired. Resigned. She says she will just wait. The crowd has to go away at some point. Right? They have to sleep. Even in New York City. Then Max Klein gets an idea. A sacrificial lamb of an idea. He drapes her boa around the sister's neck, and then puts her coat around the sister's shoulders. Drops a bouquet in the sister's lap, and tells Jarrett that the two of them should get in Madame's carriage now and begin the impersonation. Meanwhile she and Max will slip into the sister's carriage and take the quiet but expeditious ride back to the hotel.

For a moment they all sit and stare at one another. Contemplating. They are all about to become part of her theatrical production. And like the actors in her company, they wait for her to make the first move. She tries to breathe in enough energy to proceed with Max's plan. She thinks about the first night she had entered the Booth: a young girl, probably her age, wanted a signature, but the girl's pen had run dry. She could have borrowed another. Instead, the girl scratched the nib across her skin's surface and drew blood for ink. It was exhilarating and revolting. Something no one would ever want to see again. Finally Sarah lifts her tiny body. The drama is strength. She looks only at Max. She tells him that it is time to go.

Under the cover of darkness, and the willingness for belief, the crowds at the door fall for the deception. She and Max lag a few steps behind. They watch the promoter and the imposter bull their way through into the cab and proceed slowly through the crowd and into the night. At least two-thirds of the crowd follows the carriage, running and pumping a little faster as the coach gathers speed.

She and Max step unmolested into her sister's ride. They watch the traces of hysteria. In the midst of this comedy, she thinks that there is no place like America. Where the convergence of celebrity and art fall together under one footstep. Where art leads to fanaticism.

It is beauty.

A true *raison d'être*.

C H A P T E R   O N E
May 13, 1906

SHE barely noticed the blind man's cane lying by the side of the road. In fact if she were forced to describe it, Sarah Bernhardt might have said that she assumed it was white with those little red soldier stripes near the top, although she couldn't be certain. She would recall that it was unusually long, a detail she'd remember because it would seem almost impossible to lose something of that size. The crook at the top formed a handle. Other than that, the only other notable aspect was that there were two spent cigarettes beside the cane. One that had been stamped and crushed, creased by the impatient imprint of a boot's sole. The other lay smoldering. Smoked down to the end, but with a corner still bright in ember red, and a disfigured trail of smoke streaming out. It was hard to imagine that a blind man would just lose his cane. He should be stumbling around, his arms extended, fingers reaching for direction in Oedipus's fear.

She looked one way up Rose Street, then back down the other.

Empty.

She envied the thought of the mysterious blind man liberated from his cane, suddenly free to stumble and fall, with no hardwood guide clanking against metal streetlamps to keep him on track, as though he were actually seeing. She became jealous imagining his discovery of accidentally stumbling along the rough face of a concrete wall, his virgin hands feeling the intense heat and sharpened cracks. Or the feeling of his heart skipping a beat as he stepped off the ledge of the sidewalk, momentarily uncertain at the sensation of falling, only to discover the pleasure of solid ground. Everything would be new and free from constraint. He probably threw the cane away, declaring freedom for the first time in his monitored and scripted life.

What she had really wanted to do was pick up the cane and smash it through the nearest window in intense anger, rewarded by the sound of shattered glass. Instead, Sarah left the cane by the side of the road as a sign of hope, praying that the blind man didn't find that freedom was too deadly.

She tried to find a street sign. Sarah Bernhardt was sixty-one years old and again found herself walking down unfamiliar streets. She didn't want to get lost. Lord knows she was a compass with no needle. Practically blind herself outside of a theater or hotel or restaurant. She sometimes wished they would stencil in blocking patterns along every street she trudged, then she could just travel back and forth between white V'd line to white V'd line. Sarah looked over her shoulder at the King George Hotel, raising her stare until it settled on the fifth floor, just beyond halfway, to the window in the center. She wanted to make sure she had left a light on as a beacon. A North Star to guide her back. She was so furious when she had left, and she couldn't recall exactly what she had or hadn't done, other than try to kick the newspaper across the room, and when it wrapped stuck around her toe, she ripped it off and heaved it violently toward the mirror, where it sailed down in confused grace into little paper boats and tunnels. When she slammed the door, she heard the papers rustling in a discomforting little whisper. She was pretty sure she had turned on the light out of habit. She hadn't cared. All she had wanted was to get away from the room, past the doting concierge, and out into the faceless night.

She was accustomed to playing Los Angeles—where she always played—and she didn't need any beacons or stage marks to find her way along Broadway, passing theaters like the Merced, where she remembered seeing the booking on the itinerary. Today had actually started last night in Tucson, Arizona, at the tail end of a restorative two-day retreat. Max had reached her by phone, speaking with an almost conspiratorial lack of words, saying he was glad that he had found her, and that he hated having to be five hundred miles away right now. "There has been a slight change of plans," he had said.

She asked him what.

"Venice." His voice was quieter than usual, void of the routine banter.

"Italy?"

He had been kind enough not to laugh or condemn her for the obviousness of her question. That should have been the first sign. "We're taking La Dame aux Camélias up the road to Ocean Beach. Venice of America," he had said. "Things have gotten suddenly complicated in Los Angeles."

"Like what?"

"It is too much to explain by telephone, but it's all for the better, believe me. I'll be there a day and a half behind you."

"A day and a half by myself?"

"You won't even be there until tomorrow night. That's really only a day alone. I'm getting out of Santa Fe as fast as I can. But it's all set. Terms are negotiated."

"But, Molly, I need you here to run through lines."

"Marguerite Gautier's? You have said those a thousand times or more."

"It is the last part that is troubling me. The final scene. I can't manage to let the disease take her. I am too much in control of the sickness. I am giving it its life."

"You are overthinking it."

"It is a matter of control. Recently, Marguerite's consumption has lost the power and insidiousness. I just can't find it right now. The sickness just doesn't subsume me. It feels so tangible."

"I will be there soon."

"Or perhaps I am bored with it."

"We will run through that final scene as much as you need in your room."

"In my railcar?"

"You have a suite booked at the King George Hotel."

"An English place? Where is the car?"

"Once the crew arrives, we'll have your private car parked. Apparently it will work out perfectly, there are some leftover construction tracks right on the pier. You'll be able to have your privacy, and get away during rehearsals and preproduction. You do not need to worry . . ."

"You are sure my railcar will arrive? These situations tend to be accompanied by problems."

"It was a stipulation. No need to worry. You know I wouldn't keep you from your comforts. Nor would I upset the Vanderbilts' generosity."

"Dear Molly. My protector. Through all of Christendom."

"If you need anything between now and then—Abbot Kinney. Call on him. He's the proprietor of the hotel, and the whole town for that matter. He is available if you need anything."

She was beginning to dislike his seriousness. "Does this Kinney get the opium, as well?"

Max didn't say anything. In the silence there was the clicking and static of shared phone lines, and she finally gave in with a laugh and said she was only kidding.

"It wasn't funny."

"I was only trying to raise a smile from my sweet Molly."

"You just need to make it one more day."

"You are no fun today, Molly . . . I would much rather play Los Angeles."

"I'll see you in one day." The conversation had sputtered, with Max giving her the travel specifics and placating her by saying that in addition to negotiating a higher fee out of Kinney, he had also managed to arrange for her to fish off the pier the next morning. He knew how she liked to catch her breakfast, something she said that she had done every summer as a girl, and it would give her something to do until he arrived. "A day and a half," he said. "Forget about Marguerite. Use the time to rest up for the crew . . . Do a little fishing . . . It's really only a day."

This strangely clean carnival town was empty and silent. A vacant Ferris wheel arched into the sky, poking its perfect skeleton above the amusement park. She passed the large barn-shaped dance hall, the walls quieted by night, strolling by a series of rides made more mysterious by their elusive names like the whip and the Virginia reel and the Great American Racing Derby. She continued to walk toward the giant auditorium, built toward the end of the pier, the sunset leaking across its giant red rooftop. Behind her, Venice of America extended beyond the pier into streets carved and gutted into canals, where gondolas sailed throughout the day, captained by gondoliers in requisite black striped shirts and thick dark mustaches, accents thick enough to make you question your surroundings. And according to information in the lobby, minstrels strolled the sidewalks with lutes in hand, and at one corner at half-past three every day—including Sunday—the richest set of vocal cords you could imagine sang Verdi in a sweet baritone that silenced the waves. And there were brass bands and magicians and fire. "It's another world," the literature read.

Sarah pulled up on her skirt, trying to preserve the flower trim that dragged mercilessly along the dirty pier, then let it fall again. She pushed back her shirtsleeves, feeling the silk caress her skin, and appreciated the sting of the ocean breeze. She sniffed the shirt cuff, hoping to take in some remnant of the Parisian air but instead only found the staleness of stowed-away trunks and luggage cars. Her foreignness felt astounding. The artifice that permeated this California coastline in some vision of natural bliss was tragically beautiful. At once there was a sense of history without the years, freedom without the bloodshed. And life without the living. She continued to walk forward into the slowly deepening night. Her feet trembling along the fragile pier. Air thick with salt. And the lump of orange sun falling into the horizon cast a light that turned everything an otherly pale shade of pink and blue.

She made her way toward the end of the dock, past the auditorium and its ornate details and cathedral windows. She looked back over her shoulder. The King George was gone from view, leaving her comfortably lost, as though Athena's fog was set solely around her, safe in her disorientation. Now she could be as far away as possible from that hotel room and the deadly newspaper that had littered the room. Her seeing that front-page story had initially overtaken every frame of her body, as though she had been a pliable, empty form that was easily filled and imbibed by seething hatred. Her anger had spoken in a secret language of consonants and plosives that hammered against the nerves. Mostly furious. Slightly wounded. Helplessly vicious.

Coming across the newspaper was a fated accident. After checking in to the King George, she had been left standing for an interminable amount of time outside her room, leaning on a maid's cart that sat temporarily abandoned. Even with the addition of forty years, the actress had still managed to climb the stairs faster than the Mexican bellhop, who despite the weight of her trunk, still should have maintained a steady clip past her, based on the pride his shoulder muscles showed beneath his undersize coat. She felt like she had waited forever outside her door, studying the blue Victorian patterns of the wallpaper and the fresh designs the vacuum had etched in the shorthaired carpet. How long could she wait for this failed matador to wrestle her valise up to her room and unlock her door? She paced the halls, making up rules that if the next person on the floor was not the bellhop then she would stomp down the stairs, grinding each one to dust, and demand that this Abbot Kinney himself come rectify the problem. It had been in that moment when she swiped the *Los Angeles Herald* from the cart. She had unfolded it just enough to see the headline "Future of Los Angeles Theaters in Doubt," but closed it when she finally saw the struggling lackey, banging her case like it was a bum third leg. She restrained from scolding, figuring that French to English to English to Spanish was probably a fruitless effort. Instead she tucked the newspaper under her arm and stood hands on hips, with her foot tapping impatiently. Once inside the room she waved him off, only acquiescing to the gratuity by placing a quarter in his palm at the last second. His eyes had looked hungry.

She had lain down on her bed, tired and lonely. The road was exhausting. The strange places started to seem even stranger. These days she felt less and less like an actor, and more like a commodity. Maybe she had done too many farewell tours of America. Or maybe the public didn't care about an old woman, instead only going to see her in order to expand their cocktail repertoire (who even really cares that the plays are performed in French, because it is the Divine Sarah). They wanted their Sarah with an energy that burst from her eyes, a mouth that would say anything, and a radiance that outshone the moonlight. This time around she could sense the disappointment when she took the stage. In Santa Fe she swore she heard a collective silence as loud as any ovation. They were studying her, trying to find the Sarah that they adored despite the unfamiliar falling jowls and wrinkled eyes of the woman before them. Most only started to find true satisfaction by the third act when the power and intensity of her performance as Marguerite Gautier outpaced anything that the younger Sarah had ever done, a maturity that her predecessor never knew. She was beginning to hate the younger Sarah, the pretty younger sister that everybody compared her to. But in truth it was guilt. The terrible sense of having lost her. Of not having given that younger Sarah anybody to look up to.

At first the *Herald* article gave a bit of background on the Los Angeles theater district, nothing that she hadn't known (or really cared about). But her hands started to tighten and shake, her knuckles trying to break the skin, when she read her own name in the third paragraph: *Due to the boycott's apparent success, Sarah Bernhardt has been prevented from performing in Los Angeles.*

She didn't even remember all the words that were said about her, only that they were said by a Bishop Thomas Conaty of the local diocese, and one of his parishioners, some woman named Dorothy O'Brien, all under the guise of the League of Decency, a group that proclaimed its mission of preserving the values of the parish and community by preventing the surge of indecencies that would pollute the area. They spoke from downtown Los Angeles, at the Cathedral of our Lady of Angels on Second Street, but the words and quotes lashed out at her as though the bishop, this O'Brien woman, and the writer, Vince Baker, were sitting across from her, spewing their frozen words through warm, sour breaths:

She's a pied piper. A slayer of decency. Cavorting from town to town with a troupe of sin-makers, whirling in and defaming the name of goodness and God with antics that would make the devil himself blush. Causing the vulnerable people of this town to somehow forget the fulfillment of belief, and think that their curiosity and needs can be filled by the dangerous frivolity that sends messages intended to dismantle the basic moral virtues of man.

She ingested each sentence like it was a purgative meant to annihilate the soul.

Sarah Bernhardt is at the heart of this sickness. Her spirit has clearly been taken, her virtue evaporated. I swear by the Father, that she has no sense of right and wrong, no place of decency. The woman wears men's clothes, dresses up on the stage in pants, and glues beards to her face, and glorifies the basest of all human dignity. A sexual immoral. Taking partners out of wedlock. No doubt engaging in homosexuality.

As she flipped over to page eight, the story seemed to go on forever. A boycott had been waged over the past week, and despite the relatively small number of active protestors, the League of Decency had succeeded in having her Los Angeles shows canceled. "I am in the entertainment business, not the political statement business," one unnamed theater owner was quoted. "The last thing I need is attention from church ladies with picket signs."

The article did suggest that the bishop might have been furthering his agenda of relocating the cathedral to Ninth Street, where it could be a more dominant force "out of this slum." But that seemed pro forma, the writer Baker's perfunctory attempt at objectivity.

She finally lost all control when she noticed the picture of the flyer the league had used. It was crude. A brutal pen and ink sketch of a face that looked contorted and evil. It was strikingly male, with exaggerated features, accentuating the Semitic traits that flowed nearly forgotten through half her bloodstream. A nose bursting from the center. Big fat lips that appeared to have been pummeled or swollen from a bee's sting. The hair was obviously female, as chaotic pen strokes frazzled it in a big mound to the upper border of the page, then let the locks flow far past the face in rough stilted scratches. And written across the bottom: *Boycott Sarah Bernhardt and anybody who supports her. Keep Los Angeles moral. Don't commit sin. The Greater Los Angeles League of Decency.*

That was when she kicked the paper, cursing Los Angeles, the press, and the betrayal of the Catholic church, which had raised her in one of its convents. The hotel room became confining and hot, her lungs dry and flat, and her throat parched wickedly dry. And as the paper fluttered to the floor, that caricature stared right at her the whole way down, its horrid expression almost sneering. But that wasn't her. Beneath the anger she knew all along that it was the other Sarah Bernhardt. That younger version that again took all the attention, and had picked all the fights, nearly enjoying the attention and celebrity more than her art. Before she slammed the door, Sarah turned to spit on the picture. She cursed the other Sarah for what she was doing to *her* life.

It was not as if she had never fought battle after battle on American soil, defending her right to art against the puritanical fanaticism of self-made morality. But when she was younger it had had a certain air of gamesmanship to it. She did not take it so personally. Like when that Episcopalian Bishop What's-His-Name in Chicago had stood in his pulpit before God and the *Chicago Tribune* proclaiming, "Sarah Bernhardt is an imp of darkness, a female demon sent from the modern Babylon to corrupt the New World." The *Tribune* reporter had stalked her in the newly built Congress Plaza Hotel, trailed her along the green-carpeted lobby, and across Michigan Avenue into Grant Park. "Madame," he called out. "Do you have a comment on the bishop's statement?"

She hadn't heard it, and when the reporter relayed the remark, she laughed out loud, her tiny frame feeling magnified and bloated in righteousness. From the corner of her eye she had seen a horrified Max Klein, wilting at the thought of the unlikely combination of confrontation and conflict. She could see him gathering his thoughts, trying to compose an appeasing retort that would serve to diffuse the bishop's ire and keep his boss's honor intact. But as Max had tried to fumble his way through a stuttering introduction clearly meant to give his brain time to organize, Sarah literally stepped in front of him, and said to the reporter, "To the bishop, I say this: Why attack me so violently? Actors should never be hard on one another." She threw her head back and laughed, her red hair tickling her back.

Even the reporter had smiled a little. He asked if he could use the quote, looking to Max for some kind of permission, the way men always do when a woman is in the presence of another man.

"Of course you may," she said, still laughing. "And since when does a reporter ask?"

Her response had run the next morning. Max was mortified. He thought that maybe he should go to the Southern Theater to make peace with the producer, to diffuse any potential situation. Sarah told Max that he should relax. She laughed when he talked about not being able to afford a box office loss. "Now it is like a sporting match," she said to him. "People will buy a ticket just to see who takes the next blow. You watch, the house will be full. That is America." Then she told him to sit down next to her, patting the couch twice, as if calling a dog. She had spilled a little vial of cocaine on the glass tabletop and said they should enjoy this city as long as they are here. That was back in the days when Max had as much trouble resisting the spell of the drugs as she did. "One promise," he had said, tilting his head up with closed eyes, letting the drug fall into his head. "Please give an opening statement tonight to reaffirm that you are not at battle with Chicago nor its religious community." She smiled and nodded, then took her own hit.

That night, in front of the hand-painted curtain of the Venice canal, Sarah had stood at the edge of the Southern Theater's proscenium, looking up into the glowing lights that walled off the concentric arches, each seat fully filled from the orchestra to the balcony. Set alone in the footlights. She looked once stage left to see the silver silhouette of Max's tentative but encouraging nod. She cleared her throat. From her tiny body a voice pure yet forceful filled the hall, almost as though it were its own being. "First off," she said, "I thank all of you for being here tonight. Chicago is certainly the pulse of America." The audience had roared, clapping and hollering despite the scenic erudition of gowns and black ties now immediately reduced to adulating fans. Her presence was that brilliant. Then she looked back to Max once more and shrugged her shoulders, cocking her head with a whimsical smile that precluded an apology. "As far as the bishop," she began. There was already an undercurrent of laughter when she pulled a bank draft from the cleavage in her dress and bent over the edge of the stage to hand it to an elderly man with a neatly trimmed mustache. "I trust that you will give this to his Excellency and deliver this message for me," she began. "When I bring an attraction to a town," she stated, "I am accustomed to spending five hundred dollars on advertising." Then she opened her arms to acknowledge the full house. "Since your Excellency has so gratefully done half the advertising for me, I herewith enclose a two-hundred-fifty-dollar rebate for your parish." The audience had erupted into a tremendous cheer while the drop curtain rose, revealing the paint and nail streets of Paris from which Marguerite Gautier would soon appear.

But aging has a way of sucking the venom out of the fight. And you find yourself starting to slink away, not out of cowardice or onset reticence, but more from the realization of the power of the situation. And the words and vitriol carry every ounce of spite intended, and it is you who is targeted. They are not aimed for play. They are aimed for hurt. So you mostly walk away, trying to assign some meaning to the action, without taking it personally. Sometimes it makes you want to give up.

From the end of the pier, the ocean looked black, strengthening the power of the waves. These were the times when a strong hit of opium was the best solution. A moment when your head can be drained of pressures and filled with glorious truths. It held the power to whittle away the harshness of catechisms, and unblock fear at its worst moments—almost as good as being on the stage. Max worried about her abusing the drug. On occasion, he delicately brought it up in the same way that one brings up alcohol with a drunk, carefully timing it between the sober and the craving. She usually ended up angry with him, reminding him of how much he used to use, and then disappearing behind a bathroom stall where she could smoke without hassle and forget Max's judgment. But following the last lecture in Santa Fe, she had promised him that she wouldn't bring any opium in her trunk to Los Angeles. Poor Max didn't know that she had only put it in his. What a mistake that was. Three days hadn't seemed such a long way away. And she never could have anticipated knowing the intense rage that would bind to weigh upon her soul.

In the lobby of the King George, the concierge greeted her

with a polite fawning. His face showed some concern, as he had been on the blunt end of her waving hand when she had stormed out of the lobby. She smiled politely and nodded her head. The room seemed to stretch infinitely upward, with the hand-painted molding almost lost behind the twinkling glare thrown by the chandelier's constellation. The furniture was stunning; these were not a set designer's charade. The striking yellow and red velvets could only be the result of Italian craftsmanship. And seated on a love seat, plush and red with a high back and a gently carved mahogany border at the top, an old man was by himself, his gray nest hair sticking out in several directions. He leaned forward the way many lonely men do, staring out the door behind full black glasses, whittling his right index finger against his left. A strange molested smile hung on his face. She wondered if he was missing a cane.

"Did Madame enjoy her walk?" the concierge asked.

She immediately knew that he had read the article. She could see the collusion in his hard stare and nervous shoulders.

"Is there anything I can do to help make your stay more pleasant?"

She sensed that he was ushering her. On orders to keep her occupied, anything to prevent her from knowing the truth of the situation. And the thought of being in the epicenter of the secret started to infuriate her again. Where the concentric circle of deceit spun out from around her. Everybody she had met since arriving in California had figured her to be too stupid or unaware to know what was going on. A world of nameless gawkers who felt themselves privy to her darkest moment.

She looked the concierge in the eye. Her expression stern and metered, swallowing one last breath as she prepared to expose the whole conspiracy. "Yes, you can help me," she spoke in a controlled fury. "You can clear that shit of a newspaper from my room, and from the rest of the hotel, for that matter."

She smiled at the stranger in the dark glasses, then turned and walked toward the bar. Shoulders squared and proud. In full view of the other Sarah.

Purposefully not turning around to see the mask undone.

VINCE BAKER HAD BEEN GIVEN the assignment three days ago. His sonabitch editor at the city desk, Graham Scott, had told him that he had better talk to Bishop Conaty as soon as possible. They had a story to break. He was holding two page-one columns, and another half page for the jump. The rival *Los Angeles Examiner* had sucker punched them last year on the Vienna Buffet scandal, running a front-page story declaring the lack of morality of the *Herald* staff. The piece had placed *Herald* reporters at the Vienna Buffet, a restaurant of doubtful reputation, hunkered down in the underground passage with a bevy of questionable women, some of whom were called actresses, and some the *Examiner* kindly referred to as "abandoned." There were tales of booze, the drinks flowing at a modest twenty-five cents a shot, and then moved on to Mumm's Extra Dry at a hefty three dollars per pint, all billed to the *Herald* tab in the name of journalism, resulting in charges being filed by the police commissioner for selling illegal liquor. Stories flowed throughout the city newsrooms of broads on laps and under tables. And the *Herald* just couldn't get it straightened out. F. T. Seabright, one of their longstanding reporters who had been present at the Vienna Buffet, only dug the hole deeper when he tried to explain that Scott had sent him and another reporter down for an undercover investigative piece on the proffering of illegal booze. But his unnecessary details about the length and feel of the girls' thighs threw his credibility into doubt. The *Examiner* was really sticking it to their rival now, recently drawing the religious and community leaders into the drama, as was that reactionary Harrison Gray Otis of the *Times*. The *Herald* was taking it from all sides. Threats of boycotts. Letters to the editor. A cry for penance. So when this loudmouth bishop and his cohorts started making noise about the indecency of Sarah Bernhardt and their intended boycott, Graham Scott saw it as a chance to make a righteous gesture to the community at large, but more importantly to finally shut up the bullshit *Examiner* editorial staff. So he sent his best man. Someone who could make the story sing.

Vince Baker was fairly young by newsroom standards, having just turned thirty in mid-January. The old dogs in the newsroom were okay with him. They thought he had the balls of an old beat hound and they admired the grace with which he could turn nothing into something. He could make anything news. A natural at contorting information into stories where facts hung on the perimeter of truth, with a pinch of sensationalism. They loved that shit at the *Herald*. Took him off assignments like covering births at the zoo or the largest quilt ever made this side of the Mississippi and gave him the helm as their lead city man. Threw him stories right and left. Told him to chase down the rest. They fucking loved him. Slipped him fifty for a Christmas bonus. Sent him memos all the time saying, "That was great work." He was going places. He was assigned all the gritty city hall pieces. Every power broker in town knew him by face. Doheny. Harrington. Huntington. G. G. Johnson. They all hated the garbage that his paper put out, but they talked anyway because they knew Baker would write it with or without their quotes. This town was packed tight in his fist. Although he knew he was really nothing other than the modern-day version of the town crier, Baker still managed to keep a sense of integrity and pride—he honestly believed in his role in exposing the ugly underneath. And now he was given the task of salvaging the paper's reputation by burying the Vienna Buffet once and for all. Playing the pawn in a cheek-to-cheek dance where a grinding pelvis is followed by a knowing wink.

How was that for irony?

Baker did what he did best—he turned oyster shit into a pearl. He interviewed the bishop and one of his flock, Dorothy O'Brien. They snapped the picture. He talked to the theater owners. Drafted the story in a dive named Ralph's around the corner from the church and edited the commas in a downtown bar that would make the Vienna Buffet look like a family *Hof brau*. He filed the story. A goddamned hero he was around the newsroom.

After that Tuesday edition ran, Baker tossed the unread paper into a garbage can and then stopped off at a local bar named Willie's. He threw back a couple shots of some well whiskey that stung like a sonabitch. He gave a nod to the bartender and a few malcontents hugging the corner but didn't speak a word. He lifted a Lucky Strike from his pocket, tapped the butt against the mahogany once or twice, and then stuck it unlit between his lips. He leaned forward to light the cigarette by candle flame, then pulled back, smoke rising from the amber tip. Takes you right off the stinking earth with the first drag every time. He ordered up another glass. Sucked the cigarette down to the bone. Then rinsed back the whiskey.

He wasn't ready to go home. Being alone in his new apartment on Pico could be dangerous, a man could lose himself in that kind of mess, rot away crazy until the landlord finally has the doors rammed in when the unbearable stench gets too loud. But he also had no intention of pouring on a useless drunk, one that would inevitably find him stupidly waking up with the last broad left standing at closing time.

Baker slapped two bits on the bar to settle and left. The night air was still warm, smelling of Pacific salt and bubbling lard from the Mexican taco stand up the street. It seemed quiet out. A few couples strolled back in secret huddle, followed by an occasional chatty group with one inevitably shrill distaff laugh that hung nearly visible against the concrete and plaster. The oddly loud volume of his shoes against the sidewalk thudded like the trampling of lazy hooves.

He found himself walking down Second. Hands in his pockets. Integrity feeling slightly wounded. He picked up his pace. Skirting past closed offices and businesses. No sign of life other than the winking eye of a haberdasher's mannequin under a small gray-brimmed hat. Our Lady of Angels lay one block ahead. He thought to cross the street and avoid the thing altogether. He couldn't give a rat's ass about what they were doing and why. He had done his part. Played the middleman in the brokerage of decency. The one who kissed and made up, keeping a straight face while Bishop Conaty and O'Brien spewed out the most sinfully vicious thoughts. But he took it well. Wrote it up convincingly and eschewed being a reporter, instead turning goodwill ambassador for a day. But if he had had a crystal ball when he rolled out of that no-name lady's bed two mornings ago, he would have walked right into the *Herald* office with a FUCK YOU sign taped across his chest and given

the *Herald* another scandal to negotiate. He had no intentions
of turning into their gossip guy, covering people whose biggest
crises are which theaters they are going to play.

The cathedral looked set back and almost haunted under
the cover of night. Plaster fissures slowly leaked down the
wall. Each step had a pile of uncrushed leaves windswept
into the corner that made the perfect bum's pillow. A general
lifelessness to the windows, long ago absent of the fog of
human breath. Baker imagined that somewhere in the back of
the church, the bishop must have been mulling around. Maybe
preparing a sermon, decoding the fine print of a land contract,
or in one of those chats with God. Maybe Dorothy O'Brien was
still in there, poring over the roster of names for potential
league members in her head while polishing the savior's feet.
She would look up at the sound of the bishop's footsteps,
and congratulate him on his work with the reporter, silently
begging for the bishop's attention and admiration. And they
would have no idea that the reporter felt like one of the broads
he took home and banged when the bars closed—used and
alone. All potentials cast away.

Vince Baker sat down on the steps of the cathedral. He
wiped his nose against his sleeve. It smelled of tobacco. The sky
opened in purple with stars sparkling in promise. Sometimes
there is no place like Los Angeles to make you feel full of life.
Everything is believable and possible. Maybe the bishop would
walk right out the front door now. He could sit beside him, and
Baker could explain it all to the priest. Then they could gaze at
the stars together and smile, thinking about how great it is to
live in L.A.

CHAPTER TWO
May 14, 1906

ABBOT Kinney stood next to her, a crisp knuckled hand on the doorknob. His sweat smelling of the smoke that made his tobacco fortune. Sarah could barely see his eyes in the darkness of his office, a small adjunct room tucked into the bottom corner of the auditorium that adjoined the pier that bore his name. She could only imagine Kinney's tall, worldly physique by the stature in his voice.

Bright sunlight streamed in beneath the door. Beyond the dark entrance, the cries of the miniature railroad that circled the distant midway blew along the weathered planks. Heavy sea air rolled down the great incline of the auditorium's red roof and spilled onto the bustling pier, while a procession of brass entertained the sightseers on the gondolas navigating the replicated canals of Kinney's dream city: Venice, Italy.

"They're all out there," Kinney said. "Waiting for you. Go

tell them you don't care. That's what you wanted, right?" His crooked finger eerily pointed at the door. The scribes from the Los Angeles tabloids all gathered at the heart of the newly built pier. Keenly aware that the great French actress sat sequestered in the founder's office. Their shoes tapping faintly. A murmur of voices clipped by the rush of the tide breaking under the quay. There were two quotes that they expected—a flip Sarah Bernhardt denunciation filled with a sardonic yet demure tone about the Los Angeles archdiocese, and one from Kinney that disregarded the Los Angeles culture as a thing of the past, citing as an example Sarah Bernhardt's pending performance in Venice of America.

The reporters had been waiting outside for nearly a half hour. An event orchestrated by Kinney himself. A self-made publicity man, he was the type who wasn't nearly as intimidated by reporters as he was by the fear of failure. Certain that with one errant move he could trample his reputation into a fine powdery dust. This town was not kind to damaged careers. Guys like Kinney always needed to keep the business going. And show results. Otherwise it was a long slow road back to Shitbowl, New Jersey.

Kinney had wanted something big to happen with his development. He wanted people to know that he had been the one to draw a line in the beach in 1904 and declare this playland of west Los Angeles as the new entertainment center of the city. Coney Island meets Italy. Canals and Ferris wheels. Venice of America. Ocean Beach. CA. He needed an event to turn a profit for the theater. He told that to his staff every day. Told them he was paying them to make things happen. Not just agree. And last week when those loudmouth Catholics started blowing their traps about Sarah Bernhardt being immoral and unfit for performing downtown, it was Kinney who personally tracked down Max Klein in midtour in New Mexico and made the arrangements to get her here. All within a matter of hours. His next move was to make sure the whole world knew where she was and why.

VINCE BAKER HAD BEEN ORDERED by Graham Scott to wait there on the pier. Normally Scott would have assigned a story like this to an F. T. Seabright, but since the Vienna Buffet debacle, Seabright had become too gun-shy to investigate where his balls went on an cold night. Scott had tried to convince Baker this story was bigger than some petty pugilist shit. "She is as big as all those robber barons that you like to cover. She is powerful. Look at how easily she stirs up guys like Conaty."

The boycott story had made Baker sick, but the fact that he was brought into the politics of the Vienna Buffet made him even sicker. It was no different than falling for a broad at closing time. But what had really started to gall him was how Sarah Bernhardt became his beat, and his byline. There was no time for this—not when Los Angeles was in the process of turning itself inside out and unfolding into something bigger and larger than it ever might have imagined. And there were greedy millionaires lining up at the gates to claim their shares. That's where the news was. That's what he knew. Not this Seabright kind of shit. Scott was wrong—she didn't have an ounce of their power or their stature.

As he approached the entrance to Kinney's office, Baker noticed a new crew of reporters gathering. He didn't know the faces. Seabright probably would. They were the entertainment guys. Downtown boys. The ones who palmed the maître d' a brand-new bill in order to sit behind a table of celebrities. They pretended to be engaged in other activities while they listened intently, scratching notes under the table, leaning back with staged yawns, practically dropping their ears on the neighboring table when the celebrity talk turned to a whisper. Then they submitted this spying to their editors and it ran in the rags religiously with neither a confirmation nor an opportunity from the celebrity subjects to respond. The reporters never introduced themselves. Kept it cat and mouse. Chicken shit kind of stuff. But the editors loved it. Readers ate up that gossip, and it sold papers. Sold advertising. A constant reminder to all involved in the industry that the newspaper was first and foremost a business.

To a passerby, Baker would have appeared the distant one. He stood attentive near the periphery of the crowd, his eyes with the narrow pitch of a wild hunter, the near visible adrenaline pulsating against his temples. Once the action started, these social scribes would launch a couple of empty questions, laugh gratuitously at the responses, ingest whatever Kinney served up, and then turn in the story before deadline with just enough time left to throw back a few at the company watering hole before the suspicious hours loom, where husbands and bartenders are forced into a collusion of silence. But Baker wanted to get his quotes and get out. Then he might find some real news.

SARAH BERNHARDT TUGGED ON HER DRESS, brown batiste cotton with embroidered red polka dots, and an ivory lace hemline that graced the floor of Kinney's office. Her shirtwaist was a subtle white, blooming out from her straight-front corset that she defiantly wore loose at the torso, revealing the true beauty of her delicate figure. She patted the sides of her hair, and then adjusted the pink sash that adorned her head in the latest style.

"Well, then," she muttered as she sat down in a thick-framed captain's chair, the wooden dowels jailing her back. She propped her elbow up on the armrest, and rested her cheek against a loosely closed fist. Sarah looked at Kinney set with a lazy posture, his arms crossed in mock authority. She was inclined to make a pedantic remark designed to waylay his overestimation of himself but instead swallowed her comment, as bitter as the salt air. By this point in her life, she had learned some sense of control. She had met a million Abbot Kinneys before, and found their self-aggrandizing pusillanimity to be personally offensive. They didn't know what it really took to be at the top. They were usually the types who latched themselves onto some peripheral part of the chain, and hung on tight enough to feel the warmth of the spotlights. So sure that they were *in the know*. In her younger days she would have said something that reminded him of the difference between them. A quick swipe at his lanky physique, a demand that he shine her dog's ass, or determine which of her shoes stank worse. But today she didn't say anything. Once again, the other Sarah had abandoned her.

Abbot Kinney's face etched an outline shadow, his pointed beard shone in its grayness. "When you walk outside, every Los Angeles reporter is going to be waiting for you to tell him that you couldn't care less. That the great Sarah Bernhardt could give a damn about what some dementia-brained Catholic thinks about her career." He dropped his hand from the doorknob and laced it bureaucratically behind his back. Pacing. Calm with purpose. "Because I'll tell you one thing, the dirty little secret—they're not sure if you matter anymore. Not sure if the light has faded from the brightest star to ever shine down on the world. That's what they want to find out—if you still have the moxie to tell them where to go. I told your manager this, and now I'll tell you: playing in Venice turns their perceptions upside down. Sends them a sign. This is where it is. Where it all will happen. We should both get down on our goddamn knees and kiss the feet of the good bishop for divinely sending you here." He told her he knew her history of brawling with these maniacs and then advised her to go out there and just shake her head with one-quarter smile, and three-quarters French indignation.

She took a deep breath. Her strength was aged and abused. She was too old for this nonsense. Sixty-one years. Her whole career had been about holding up mirrors, pursing her lips to blow the smoke away, and in the clearing creating a performance that allowed the world a chance to see a reflection of itself. Now she was exhausted. If the goddamn church wants to run her out of town, then maybe she should let them. At least she could use the rest.

"Madame, are you ready?"

She spoke softly. Her accent drowning her words in an inaudible sorrow. "I don't know what you want me to say. Tell me the script." She needed Max now. He was the only one who could run through lines with her.

"Okay, Madame," he said, "here's what you say. You say, 'I am thrilled and delighted to have the opportunity to perform at the Chautauqua at Abbot Kinney pier as part of my farewell tour of America. I am'—here comes the subtle kicker—'a firm believer in promoting culture, not restraining it. I am honored to play in Venice of America, the new center of California's cultural renaissance.' What do you think?" Kinney asked. "The beauty of it is that you thumb your nose at the cowardice of the Los Angeles theater world without ever actually thumbing. It can only reflect better on Venice. Plus it's what those reporters are all waiting to hear from you." He looked at Sarah, the diluting dark starting to turn his features accessible. The shape of his face looked tired and calculating. "What do you think?" he asked again.

"Do you have a back door?"

"Why?"

"I'm ready to go fishing."

Kinney cracked an understated laugh. A slight tearing at the sides of his mouth that tugged his whiskers. He looked controlled. Always controlled.

"I am hungry," she said. "Too hungry for all this. I just want to take a fishing pole, drop the line into the ocean, and hook a nice fish for my breakfast . . . Max said you would . . . Your chef can prepare it for me, right?"

"Of course." Kinney paused and leaned back on his desk, scattered in papers and signatures. "But I'm concerned about the press waiting for you."

"They will follow. Reporters never go away. They are just dogs led by the scent of another dog's ass. They cannot control it."

"They can't sleep until they know that they're keeping someone else awake all night." He laughed, looking over at her. "Okay, then, well, to hell with them. They come to us. Yeah? *Madame Bernhardt says that she prefers to go fishing now.* You show them the beauty of Venice of America. I'll make the announcements and then join you on the pier. We're in charge here."

A pause held the room. It felt the same as the first day she had walked into the Grandchamps convent in Versailles still as Henriette-Rosine Bernard. A scared little girl surrounded by red velvet and brass, a smirking Jesus hanging at the end of the great hall, welcoming and despising. A Mother Superior who played host and talked comforts and hypotheses. She said theories couldn't replace action. The young freethinking conscripts who came to her convent would have to give in eventually to the peace of conformity. Just be honest with God. He won't let you down. The church was after Sarah back then, as well. They didn't even bother to find the Jewish blood that traveled her veins. Maybe because they figured that her father must have money. A bank account answers a lot of prayers, so you don't even think to ask the questions. Still, she nearly gave in and became a nun. The need for belief and acceptance usually go hand in hand.

When Kinney cracked open the door for a look, Sarah heard the familiar bray of reporters jumping over one another, trying to pitch the big question. *What did she think of the bishop? I got an afternoon deadline.* Dangling ropes for the hanging. She stood up from her chair. Swallowing. Looking to Kinney. Adjusting the pink sash on her head. Her shoulders squared in a stage posture. Feet tingling. Her hands formed a dramatic pose. She still mattered. "I need to go," she said to Kinney. "Now."

Before he left, Kinney picked up the phone and instructed one of his minions that once Sarah had her catch, to bring her back to the dining room at the King George, wrapped fish and all. Louis should gut and fry it for her. Then they would figure their strategy of how to work the press and keep those loudmouth downtown Los Angeles Catholics out of Venice of America. Crucify the lousy pope if need be. He flung open the door, then closed it as quickly, leaving a flash of light that hung in the room like a frozen lightning rod.

SHE SAT WITH A FISHING POLE in her hand. Her bare legs dangled off the Venice pier. The sky was see-through blue, with the stiffed winged gulls like shadows against the horizon. Sarah pretended she sat alone, ignoring the U-shaped crowd that had gathered out of curiosity around the reporters on the dock. No doubt they were craning their necks and bobbing over one another's heads to steal a glimpse of the star. Looking out into the expanse of the Pacific Ocean, she kept her back to them as they crept up on the auditorium.

Her line sunk far beneath the water's surface in the hope of seducing an unsuspecting fish. She sometimes swayed the rod from side to side in order to create some variety, feeling the force of the water mass in its resistance. Closing her eyes. The crisp moist air blowing off the waves reminded her how small she really was in the world.

She thought that she felt a tug on the line, and her body tensed in excitement and pleasure. She centered her weight. Braced her arms. Adopted a grimace that was more anticipation than anything else. By the time she gripped her free hand on the handle for support, the line loosened, then as quickly slackened, reinstated to its former free-floating form. Such is the drama of fishing. In this constant give-and-take, unpredictable rhythm, and seat-edged suspense, Sarah felt whole. The performer and the audience at the same moment. The combustible relationship of energy between actor and viewer that sparks the theater is alive in every act of fishing. Here there is no celebrity, no cues, no critics.

Here every bit of business is stage business. With no need to jump and shout and lift her skirt bare ass in public in order to be seen. The same wholeness she felt when she would sit on crushed grass at her uncle Faure's farm in Neuilly, dragging a line across the lake, each little movement breaking and rustling the dried brown stalks, and causing the fish to scatter, leaving only a constellation of bubbles and ripples. She could sit out there all day long without catching a fish. Just gazing into a sky animated by silky clouds, unable to dream a better life.

Her line pulled again. Jerky in stilted movements. She didn't feel the usual tugging and fighting. Almost as though the catch had given itself up in a desperate attempt of hopelessness and soulless resignation. Then came a sudden force that lightened momentarily before turning heavy again. She leaned back, rolling her shoulders toward the pier. The ends of her dark hair caught in the breeze. She opened her legs for balance and strength. Stomach muscles taut and ready. Slowly cranking the fly. Reeling it in. Hoisting the catch above the surface, a fish in sequin scales, oddly content, with barely a trace of distress or fight. At least a foot long, and plump with fat.

Behind her a staccato of hands clapped from the mouth of the pier. A whoop and holler. But she didn't look back, this was not her audience. Instead, Sarah reeled in the fish, watching it come closer and closer. And as she looked into the rainbow prisms of its skin, Sarah remembered a dark winter afternoon when the Mother Superior held a manuscript that the old woman herself had handwritten. A play. A parable. *Tobie Recouverant la Vue.* Where the son of a blind man kills an evil fish. An ever-watchful angel then descends to tell the son to gut the fish and to pray religiously over the innards. In the final act, at the direction of the angel, the fish's entrails are rubbed over the eyes of the blind father to give him sight, and the angel, having turned evil into a good purpose, ascends back to heaven. Mother Superior had read her play out loud with spite and vengeance, smiling piously at the end when the goodness of God's work was brilliantly revealed through the angel's deed.

ABBOT KINNEY HAD WANDERED BACK to the crowd, rubbing elbows with the reporters, addressing the ones he knew by their first names, and nodding feigned smiles to the unfamiliar. He reiterated all the pabulum that had comprised his announcement about Venice's defining moment, leaving little time for questions about Sarah Bernhardt and why she was on the pier, other than to say, "You would be too. Like everything else, the fishing is great here in Venice." Baker stood back and listened. He had read Kinney as being smart, certainly more so than most of the reporters surrounding him. He had a stature similar to Edward Doheny, powerful and firm, with a presence that commanded attention. However, unlike Doheny, Kinney clearly wanted the spotlight.

Kinney was shooting the breeze with an *Examiner* reporter named Johnson, bragging how he had hired a couple of wetback kids to tread water beneath the pier, then swim out and hook a fish from the King George kitchen onto Bernhardt's line. He didn't want her leaving empty-handed, nor with any regrets about Venice of America. He laughed when he said that it didn't cost him anything. They were a couple of Mexican dishwashers from the hotel; the rest was implied. He lowered his voice as he leaned closer to Johnson, "I don't want to see any of this in print. If Bernhardt were to find out . . . She's a real ballbuster, that one."

Just then Kinney caught Baker's eye. "Well, I'll be. Vince Baker. Venice of America ought to pay you a commission for sending Bernhardt our way. You and the goddamn bishop. We might still be struggling if it weren't for your story."

Baker thought of saying something like "glad I could help" but resisted anything other than a perfunctory smile. There was often a power struggle between reporters and subjects as to who was going to subjugate themselves first, all dependant on how badly one needed the other. But these battlegrounds had their own castes, and while Baker and Doheny might engage in the ongoing gentlemen's duel, Baker was not inclined to lower himself to a second-tier upstart like Kinney. But still he tried to be polite. At this point Kinney was the more likely to get him the facts for an over-and-done-with story.

Baker nodded. "Is she giving interviews today? You letting her talk for herself?" He tried to keep his tone matter-of-fact. He did not want any suggestion of deference, or worse, that they were equals setting the abacus for a future of tabulated negotiations.

"She's a little busy, can't you see? You have the quotes."

"Still I'd like to hear what *she* has to say."

Kinney pursed what little lips he had between his mustache and beard, and nodded. "If you want to hear from her, then I'll be glad to set you up with a good seat on opening night. Do you prefer orchestra or balcony? I don't need the kind of news that you make."

Baker ignored him and looked out at Bernhardt, sitting almost childlike on the pier. Her shoulders slightly hunched, head dropped, with her hands gripped high on the pole. Except for the brilliance of the scarf on her head, she appeared ordinary, without mystique or fascination. A woman in her sixties who seemed as likely to single-handedly demolish the mores of Los Angeles as she was to lick her fingertips and reach out over the horizon to extinguish the sun. "Look at this crowd," Baker said. "There must be fifty people lined up behind us. Just to watch her fish. Incredible what some people will buy into."

"And you can see that she is most delighted to be here. That downtown boycott may have done her a favor, but the people of Venice are the beneficiaries."

"Come on, Kinney. Just give me five minutes."

"Orchestra or balcony?"

Baker watched Bernhardt fish. Her body swaying slightly with the breeze. She looked solid. Firmly rooted to the dock. Balanced. But one errant gust, Baker figured, could topple her over and shatter her into a thousand pieces.

KINNEY STRODE TO THE END of the dock, following his slap and tickle with the reporters. He wore straight-legged linen trousers that bunched full at the waist, a white shirt that clung to the bloat of his body, and an understated tie that traveled the contours of his midriff. He knelt beside Sarah, as much as his legs would allow. Eyes squinting in the sunlight.

She looked up at him, then turned away from the immediate boredom that he inspired, and finished bringing in her fish.

"I see you caught one," Kinney said, sounding not fully surprised.

"You are a very astute man. I should think you'll go places."

He smiled and then coughed to clear his throat. "We'll get that fellow cooked up for you right away. You're quite an angler."

The fish lay still on the deck. No flopping or fighting. One black eye round and protruding, looking upward. The end of the glistening silver hook poked through the side of its cheek, stained by a patch of blood. Sarah dropped the pole to her side. "I have never seen a fish so resigned before," she said.

"I'd say you caught yourself a sea bass," Kinney said. He leaned forward a little more to inspect the catch. "That would be my guess."

She ignored him.

"Chef Louis can do amazing things with a fish."

She propped herself up on her knees and crawled to the bass, pulling on the line to drag the fish closer to her. She crooked her index finger into its limp mouth, delicately wriggling the hook, then slid it out like a jeweled earring. The thin steel dropped against the wood. In silence.

"Madame Bernhardt, you don't need to trouble yourself with the messy stuff. Chef Louis . . ."

She took out her room key from the King George. Long and thin, with sharp jagged cuts, and hooked to a metal-banded slip of paper with the number 511 handwritten in the middle. She rolled the fish to the side. Then placed the tip of the key just below its neck. Catching the sunlight.

"No need to soil yourself." Abbot Kinney's voice trembled for the first time. His hands grabbed with no true sense of purpose or direction. He looked back to the crowd at the end of the dock.

Sarah pierced the skin with her key. The flesh popped, and a thin clear fluid washed over her hands. A stale, saltwater smell followed an outpouring of heavy syrup. She drew in a deep breath. Her grip tensing around the makeshift blade. To imagine that anybody would challenge the morality of her life. Especially in the name of God. The same God that she had nearly married. Prayed to. Paid penance. And even had her soul, half Jewess and all, cleansed in his holy water. Accusations destroy and damage. Like a stray bullet fired from hatred straight into her heart.

She drew her hand forward, ripping an incision that seemed more of the genus *mutilation*.

"Madame Bernhardt, there are reporters back in the crowd." His pleas were lost against the siren chirps of vigilant gulls.

"It is amazing that they can see the dimness of this star."

She wasn't originally cast in *Tobie Recouverant la Vue* those fifty-odd years ago. But she had begged. The Mother Superior told her that she was too pure and withdrawn to get on a stage and act. That her meekness was a virtue. Something she had interpreted as recognition of her closeness to God. "I could play the fish," she had suggested with a trace of desperation in her tone. "You can wrap me in paper. Paint it. I can bring it to life so that the angel's work seems more meaningful."

The Mother Superior had bowed her head. Her eyes softened then turned strict. Almost manlike. "You will not be given a part in the play. We have assigned a dog to play the part of the fish. He'll walk on, then walk off. It is that small."

"But I want to—"

"You don't need to be in the spotlight. Stay fragile for God."

Sarah could not make eye contact with the nun. She had turned on her heels and walked down the red stretch of carpet that rolled atop the marble floor. The eyes of a dozen Jesuses looking down on her. Knowing the Mother Superior didn't understand. She didn't get it. Sarah did not want to be cast in the play from vanity, or even as a public declaration of her faith. She wanted to feel the power of the angel. To experience the true strength of God that poured through that fish into the blind man's eyes. To feel some connection of spirit. That's all.

Abbot Kinney's complexion turned pale. He edged back a step and averted his stare away from the fish carnage. "Madame Bernhardt, please. The kitchen staff has graciously offered . . ."

She looked up at him. Her hands still hewing the fish. A thumb slipped beneath the skin, reverently stroking. "Then help me gather my things, would you. Be a good boy."

Kinney straightened up and looked back to the crowd slowly inching their way up the pier in line with the auditorium. His hands turned jittery. He scooped up the fishing rod. The line swung. The silver hook glowed, then dangled capriciously at his loafers.

"You're not doing me much good just standing there." She spoke without looking at him. Her hands now cleaving the fish's belly into two halves.

Kinney wrapped the line around the pole, securing it with the hook. He tapped the butt of the rod against the pier, and then checked back to the crowd. He sighed. He looked down to see Sarah cradling her face in the fish's innards. Her nose and mouth engulfed. The bass's body spread like open wings across her cheeks. "For the love of god."

The insides were warm against her skin. She swore the heart still pumped. Stomach grinding. Its lungs pressing for air. Blood and fluids that reeked of life on the edge of decay pooled across her cheeks, then leaked in slow streams down to her neck. Nearly fifty-three years later she has finally played in Mother Superior's *Tobie Recouverant la Vue*. But she has been cast as neither the fish, nor the angel, nor the blind man, nor his son. Instead she has played all the parts in a one-woman show. Rocking back and forth on her knees. The eviscerated bass held taut to her face as she tries to gain sight. To understand some face of God.

THE CROWD GASPED. Boots and shoes inched forward. One could almost hear the scribble of reporters' pencils. There was a contemplative silence, as though most people were still trying to decipher what they were witnessing. Maybe the light was playing tricks. Baker stood on his tiptoes, vying for more detail. He watched as Abbot Kinney fruitlessly positioned himself between the heathen and the onlookers. A stupidly long eclipse with a fishing pole in his hand, looking helpless and unusually voiceless.

But Sarah obviously heard the anticipation of the audience. She twisted her torso so that her face had peered around Kinney's frame, the fish mask cupped over her nose. Then she rolled her eyes with a tragicomic smile up to the sky where just a wisp of cloud hung lightly, in order to both bring about a laugh, and also to reassure her fans of her character's confidence.

Baker almost laughed out loud at the defiant clown who at once mocked and acquiesced. The precision timing, the exact body language, an expression contorted for effect without being prey to exaggeration. He had never seen her before, hadn't ever really known much about her before the bishop's wrath, but he always had a slight admiration for public defiance. In her small act, he could see her commitment to her art, and her extreme confidence in herself. In watching her on the pier, one wouldn't ever suppose the intense controversy surrounding her and its cancerous effect on body and soul. But as she turned slightly to the right, Vince Baker was able to see both her eyes, shaped like turned acorns, pupils like wilted buds, and in them he recognized the gem of celebrity. One that twirls in the spotlight of the sun, hoping to catch all the rays that will burst it into one startlingly magnificent light for all the world to see. He almost left. He didn't have time for that shit.

WITH A SLIGHT CHUCKLE from the crowd, followed by some scattered hand-claps, Kinney exclaimed, "Jesus Christ, you're killing me with this craziness," in the same voice of all those self-indulgent, where-are-they-now directors who schemed to keep her off the stage because true talent always threatens the stability of mediocrity.

Sarah fell out of view from the crowd with the drama of Hamlet's last breath. Her fall braced by her free hand. The fish was turning deadly and rancid. Its soul long ago risen. The scales turned stiff and prickly. She slid the bass from her face, wiping its grayish remains with the sleeve of her blouse, and threw the spent carcass at Abbot Kinney's dancing feet. She closed her eyes for a moment, then opened them to the purity of the Pacific. The rich blue. Staggered whitecaps stapled across the water top. Mother Superior's parable had come true. It took all those years to finally find the truth in her play beyond the dramatic verisimilitude. But here she lay, evil turned pure, and the blindness gone. Finally able to see.

She closed her eyes again to imagine herself now walking back into the Grandchamps convent in Versailles. The reds are still brilliant. Despite the age in her legs she still feels the same sense of fear and anticipation that she had the first time she entered as the nearly nine-year-old Henriette-Rosine. Mother Superior strides down the corridor. She hasn't changed. A nose too large for her face. Cursory black eyes set back beneath the wrinkles. A figure stout and resolute, both womanly and sexless at once. She comes up and takes her pupil's hand. "You understand what it is to see now?" she asks.

Sarah nods her head.

"What it means to anticipate what other people think of you."

Again she nods.

"That you don't need to think about those people, because God won't let you down."

Sarah moves back in nimble steps. Her bones ache. Her jaw is tired. She bites down on her lip. She can almost taste blood.

"You look unsure, Henriette-Rosine." Mother Superior's voice echoes through the great hall. "You can demur to his embrace."

Sarah's fingers roll into a clenched fist. She feels her carotid artery start to fill her neck in pride and valor. The wind takes hold of her chest in a stopped-up bellow. "I suppose I don't believe it anymore," she declares. "And I'm not sure I ever did."

The Mother Superior places her hand over her mouth, for one moment looking damsely.

Sarah kneels beneath the Mother, fixed in the spotlight. Keenly aware of the hush over the room. Her eyes welling between the fine line of performance and depth of character. Her voice is calm and modulated, almost a whisper, but at once projected from the strength of her chest. "I don't play fragile and meek very well." She looks up with a sad smile that trembles off her bottom lip. "I have only ever been successful by my strength. My truth is strength. And I cannot demur nor diminish myself on the trial of faith. It has never worked for me, and it still doesn't."

Mother Superior leans forward and cradles Sarah's head against her breasts. "God will still watch over you. And wait."

The image of the convent quickly faded away as Sarah opened her cleansed eyes to see the crisp blues and browns of the pier. The warmth of the Mother's bosom turned to the cheek-slapping chill of Abbot Kinney's face in horrid disproportion with the gutted fish at his feet, flies crawling along the innards.

Yes, God is watching over her. In the form of Bishop Thomas Conaty from the Cathedral of our Lady of Angels on Second and Main in downtown Los Angeles. Holed up in the dark rectory, no doubt a thin white candle streaming shadows along the redwood walls, transcribing the messages of evil and debauchery that face the world. Clearly led by the challenge of the demon immorality of Sarah Bernhardt and her French depravities, which have come to pollute the United States, and maybe the rest of the world, and how to ensure them from not scathing the soul of Los Angeles. At least not under his watch. Now the good bishop has taken this eye of God and entrusted its vision to his flock. And as a weapon he has instituted the League of Decency, loaded with sins and purgatories to control the insurgents. Keep the entire Los Angeles basin pure.

Bishop Thomas Conaty.

The League of Decency.

The *Los Angeles Herald*.

Abbot Kinney.

God is surely watching over Sarah Bernhardt. Waiting.

"Let's go," she ordered Kinney. Her eyes teared in defiance. She marched past him, nearly knocking the pole from his hand. Her face shining from the glaze of fish guts. Her bangs matted to her forehead. Thick tears of bloodied fat smeared along her blouse. Her stare trained above the crowd that was at once horrified and respectful. Past the reporters who held impotent pencils and would save their questions for one another over tumblers of scotch at a late-afternoon lunch, who by day's end would look willing to crawl away into the darkness and die alone.

Sarah Bernhardt turned to Abbot Kinney, who lagged conspicuously behind as she passed through the silent procession. "Let's go. I'm hungry."

C H A P T E R T H R E E
May 15, 1906

SEATED in his high-backed chair, Abbot Kinney kicked his feet up high on his desktop. Each time he shifted, a new tumble of papers fell from his desktop, drifting until they settled into the same corner beneath a dusty old cobweb. He didn't care. He never really looked at most of that stuff twice. Stupid memos, requests, unimportant correspondence. The information he really needed he kept in his head, and what was too big for his memory he stored in a locked pine cabinet. Today's newspapers sat piled on the floor. His picture on the front page of each. Four stacks of ten. Lined from the edge of his desk to the chair.

Kinney had been expecting Sarah Bernhardt for the last twenty minutes. Her entourage had not reached Southern California yet; they were still on a train that was probably in a slow-moving crawl across the Sonoran desert. But her manager,

Max Klein, had joined her late last night, and this morning the two of them began a walk-through of the Chautauqua Theater in order to get a feel for it. But they had quickly rushed out, with Klein strangely saying that he and Sarah would meet Kinney at his office in just a moment.

Max Klein was described as German but seemed to speak with something of a cultured British accent, a regular poof (and Kinney had heard Sarah call him Molly during private banter) in his permanently attired gray knobby sack suit probably tailored with its tightly tapered trousers from the London Clothing Co. Kinney had run into Max's type when he had studied and lived abroad from his early teens to middle twenties. He knew poofs like Max from his days at the University of Heidelberg who adopted stern, serious faces while hiding behind dorm room doors in frightened superiority, relegating their entire ensembles to dark black. In Paris, though, the poofs swished around with mock authority, gestured a lot with pointed fingers, and haunted all the arts venues as flighty as the falling autumn leaves. Max was a hybrid. He had a dark sophistication about him that seemed immensely private, yet his voice and mannerisms, modulated and melodic, were overtly gregarious. Max was succinct yet gracious when Kinney had let them into the theater. A hint of charm and a dash of spite. His manner took Kinney back to the good old days in Europe, before tobacco, where he spent his middle years selling Sweet Caporal hand-rolleds all over the South, and Egypt, and Macedonia. It was a long time ago. Every once in a while a flit of light gave him a glimpse of his past. The time when all that mattered was possibility.

SARAH AND MAX had been unsure about presenting *La Dame aux Camélias* in Kinney's theater. The space seemed a little roughshod despite its newness, and there was definite concern that there might be an acoustical battle with the evening ocean breezes and waves that would slap the pier's foundation. Upon first peek through the doorway, Max had uttered that it would be easier to stage the show at the Coliseum in Rome. He gave way to silence, probably understanding that there was little choice in terms of venues. The task now would be to make it work. Sarah had been remarkably quiet. She didn't appear to be studious or introspective, more as though she was the odd member. She wore a bronze silk dress with bright white stripes that cut the shoulders, with a large boa wrapped around her neck. Her feet peeked out in pointed black boots. Sarah's face was pale, void of the usual paint. When Kinney had left them, she wandered up to the balcony, moved in slow sidesteps down the upper aisle, and dragged her fingertips along the edges of the seat backs. When she reached the end of the aisle, she traversed the route one row down. That's when Kinney slipped the key to Max. He said he would wait in his office. Give them privacy to "work their magic."

Max walked Kinney to the side exit, a narrow hallway where they stood before the closed door. It smelled of damp night. Max tapped his shoes heel-toe, kicking the edge of the wall.

"I assume the theater is satisfactory?" Kinney asked.

"Still under review. We'll leave her here a while. Madame has to grab hold of it."

"She shouldn't be left alone. Reporters are crawling on their bellies looking for quotes. I think that yesterday's little stunt should be warning enough. It made every paper except one. If you don't give them head-on controversy here, then they will always go for the strange. A little more of her classic fire would probably help to offset the event."

"For the future, please do not arrange any public events without first going through me. Otherwise, Madame prefers to handle things her own way."

"Her troubles with the Comédie-Française have been well documented. Seems she has been known to be a little fiery."

"You couldn't possibly know the potentials."

Kinney smiled. "My only real concern is that Madame Bernhardt is comfortable with her surroundings." He ran his hands through his pockets, crumpling the tan linen trousers. "But she must be careful. She can't just go around performing for reporters every time she sees something she doesn't like. They will eventually kill her in this town for that, especially considering the new bloodletting craze the papers have here, and the conservative plague that's been killing us here. And you think the fucking Catholics are crazy . . . She got off lucky. I think our better strategy is to go back to her old verbal sparring. It's safer but is still likely to keep us newsworthy." He pushed the door open. A flash of light burst over the hall, rolling in like a welcome mat. He peered his head out, looking side to side, then stepped back in, leaving the door open. "Fresh cool sea air."

"Yesterday will not happen again if you leave her to me."

"It's just that I know how this town runs. I know what to do for Madame Bernhardt."

She appeared behind them. A rainbow shadow outlined her figure. "Please tell, I would very much like to know." Golden sunlight glowed through the strands of lightened hair piled atop her head. "Please continue. I'm dying to know." Her eyes looked glassy, larger than usual. Her stare seemed to take in the whole room without any of the detail. "Do tell all," she said. "And make it saucier than a dime-store novel. Perhaps a church can wage war on our heroine, with everybody in the village knowing about it except for her. Imagine the dramatic irony. The tension, and the pity." Then she laughed. Purely for herself. "But how would it end?"

Max jumped back in alarm. He grabbed Sarah by the arm and quickly whisked her out the door. "Let's continue this in just a moment," he muttered to Kinney. "We'll meet you in your office." He slammed the exit door shut. Max noticed Kinney taking notes with his eyes, scribbling every last detail to memory.

Max held on to her arm and pulled her to an inlet on the pier between the building entrances. They stepped over a strip of sunlight into the shadows. A wave broke beneath their feet, echoing far below the weathered slats. There was a rancid smell, like something had curled up and died in the corner. It was an overwhelmingly bitter and foul pungency that slowly turned sweet as fresh fruit. Max hardly noticed. He was still gripping Sarah's arm. To a passerby it might have looked like a quarrel, or even a shakedown.

Sarah shook her arm free. "But I wanted to hear what he had to say."

Max clenched his fists, and then unclenched them. Eventually he settled on shoving his agitated hands into his pockets. He bit down on his lip, and looked her in the eye. Then looked away as quickly to the thin view of ocean beneath his feet.

"Are you ready to work out the final scene with me? That room cannot handle it."

He didn't respond.

"Right now it is almost as though Marguerite is responsible for the disease. As if the tuberculosis is the knife guided by her own hand. As though she has brought on the disease only to create this tragedy of love."

Max chewed on his lip while grinding his toe between a space in the slats.

"Max, you are not listening. You are upset about something. Why is my Molly upset?"

"You think this all just comes so easily, don't you?" His voice was trembling. "Just wave a magic wand and *poof*."

"Are we bringing you into it now?" She smiled. Her eyes crinkled at the corners, without tears. "Do they still say *poof*? Or is *queer* the in slang?"

"Sarah, you are supposed to be preparing for the show. Not off in your dreamland."

She leaned forward and threw her arms around him, leaning her full weight against his chest. She touched her lips to his ear. "I love my Max so much. How he looks out for me. And sometimes I wish I could have all of my Max. But then, I suppose, I probably wouldn't love you anymore."

He felt the dryness of her breath tumbling down his neck. He didn't push her away. Instead he hugged her and held tight, listening to the breaking waves and the distant carnival sounds. The boa tickled. He massaged his knuckle beneath her shoulder blade, a sharp hand-sculpted fin. "Sarah, the hop will destroy your career," he whispered. "And you."

"*The hop*. Listen to you. *Hop*. You become so pedestrian when you come to America. Say its right name, Max. For me."

"If saying *opium* will make you stop, then there I've said it. Please." He rubbed her shoulder a little harder.

"Your touch is always perfect. That's why I love my Molly. He always cares for me."

"We won't have to worry about the Catholics if the newspapers get hold of this. You'll be run out of America in a matter of minutes. And I'll remind you that you cannot afford that in the least."

"It's not illegal."

"In fact it is here. Very illegal. Laws have changed."

"Then just tell them I have a cough. Or that I'm teething." She laughed. "Tell anybody who wonders that I've just had a nip of Godfrey's Cordial. Or Coke-Cola."

"You can't let Kinney suspect. He's the type who will look for any advantage to grab control of this situation . . . Good god, we need to air you out. That smoke smell can last for hours. I wish you had never married Jacques Damala."

"It was only for a year, my sweet."

"A year that introduced you to a culture of drugs."

"Do you remember New York, Max?"

He heard footsteps milling down the pier behind them. A woman's deep voice moaning and talking. Max held Sarah tighter to shelter her from view until they passed.

"Don't tell me you don't remember New York? And that was long before the Greek Damala."

"There have been many New York trips," he answered dismissively, hoping not to engage her. "Abbot Kinney can't even suspect, Sarah. He'll turn us into one of his junk heap circus rides. It will make a mockery of your career."

"You are my protector, Max."

"This is serious."

"Booth's Theater. Does that ring a bell?"

"Sarah. Not now."

"New York. Booth's Theater. What was that, about 'eighty? Down in the Tenderloin."

"Not long enough ago," Max sneered.

"Oh please, Molly. We took that ship over that bounced up and down the entire way. We couldn't walk straight. That was the ship that Lincoln's widow was on board. She looked tragically horrible. Gray skin. Her eyes sunken and pale. Almost a vagabond. She would have died if I hadn't grabbed her arm. The stairs were *that* steep. She knew it. She said it would have been a blessing to die. I still feel the buzz that went through me while holding her hand. Life and death all around her at the hands of actors. I didn't tell her my name. I couldn't even look her in the eye. We didn't see her the rest of the trip, did we?"

Max laughed. "Not for trying, Sarah. You spent the rest of the days trying to point her out to me until we landed at New York Harbor with all those WELCOME THE BERNHARDT signs."

"That promoter Jarrett was such an embarrassment to me. An ass."

"But he paid us well for that, Sarah. And ensured that you were the toast of the town."

She brushed him off with a wave of her hand. "The reporters all wanted to know what religion I was. Here I thought that they would be asking questions about Dumas writing *L'Etrangère* especially for me. About bringing the French craft to the United States. Or if I'd be starting off the tour with *Phèdre* or *Hernani*. No, puritan America just wanted to make sure I had some religion. I should have just copped to something. Then maybe I wouldn't have seemed so immoral to them."

"Things haven't changed much."

"But Booth's Theater. Do you remember?"

"All the customs men waiting at the theater hoping to levy a tax on the stage production." Of course he remembered. It had been his first trip to America. Every moment had seemed important. "They looked at the dresses. Each and every one. Admiring the beads and jewels."

"And you were such a frightened Molly. Just like you are now. Afraid that they would find my little canister of opium. Almost one hundred dollars' worth on that trip. You were ghostly in the corner. Couldn't even enjoy the sight of all these burly government men holding dresses up to their barrel chests."

"A different kind of fear."

"And you told me to get rid of it. As soon as they left, you said we had to get rid of it."

He grinned. She had successfully, as always, brought him into her world. Pretty soon Max was likely to completely forget the volatility of the current situation and participate in its explosion, until somebody (undoubtedly him) inevitably cleaned it up on hands and knees in the final hour. "That was a different time, Sarah. The world was a different place then."

"It was you who said that we had to smoke it. You didn't suggest throwing it over the Brooklyn Bridge or dropping it into the toilet. You said we should smoke it. And you were the one who figured out how to get us into Chinatown."

"Something like that. But Sarah let's not lose track of where we are now."

"*Whatever we do*, you said, *don't waste it.*"

It was true. Max had ordered that directive. He got directions from one of the stagehands, who asked him why they would want to go down there, and Max had said it was for the food. The stagehand said he would go with them, he'd probably be down there anyway. Max told him not to bother. He then dragged Sarah along Forty-second Street past the hobos and the destitute. Her fur coat like a shield. Whores lined the streets, stationed like soldiers, jockeying position to be closer to casino doors. Through the muck of the street, and the rotten smell of the gutters, where each open doorway smelled of either liquor or vomit. He held her tight. Protecting her. But her gait was soft and easy, and she wasn't bothered at all. Max had thanked god that they were not in Paris or London because there the diva would have been instantly recognized, and while he would have insisted on a cat-and-mouse escape, she would have stopped and bathed in the celebrity, touching hands and thanking them until she stumbled home drunk from adulation. But here, a month before opening night on her first American tour, she was just another faceless shadow, without the incessant publicity of the promoter. They took the Second Avenue El as instructed, rising high above the city in a tremolo of steel industry, the rattling vibrating his nerves while she peered out the window in excitement at the city below her. They got off at Canal Street lost and feeling especially foreign. He held her can of dope. She held his hand. Feeling exclusively endangered, they walked up past Centre Street. Max flagged down a motorized taxi and crawled into the buggy, shouting directions to the driver seated above them. "Take us somewhere where we can eat," Max said, leaving it at that. The hack tooled around until he stopped abruptly and called out, "Mott Street. Can't do better than this," knowing full well what two poshees were doing in Chinatown after sunset. He wished them good luck as he accepted the fare and reminded them of the tip. Once out of the car they were surrounded by the bustle of Chinatown. Overwhelmed by the sweet greasy smell of roasted duck, spent tobacco, and the bitterness of burning opium. Two Europeans spotlighted against the blackened street, oblivious to the gang wars and yellow peril that the newspapers warned about. They walked aimlessly up the sidewalks, pushing through the hordes of Chinese, looking for someplace to sneak into and smoke down their stash in peace. Coming around the corner Max saw the stagehand, who waved when he greeted them. "If this isn't a coincidence," the young boy said. "Something tells me you're not here to eat."

Sarah smiled from habit.

Max took him by the arm and pulled the boy in closer for a whisper. "And neither do you. Especially judging by your bloodshot eyes. Did you follow us here?"

"I was hoping I would run into you. I can set you up. I know enough China talk."

"Sarah?" Max inquired. "Do you trust him?"

By now she was in awe of her surroundings. Inhaling the dirty sidewalks; glittering in the gilded Cantonese characters that hung from the storefront above them. Sarah twirled in place, entranced by the mysticism and by her foreignness. "Sure," she replied. "He's one of us, isn't he?"

On the sidewalk, the stagehand introduced himself as Nick Brown. A native New Yorker and a regular Booth man. And while he had never known Booth, Mr. Booth's wife and daughter would know him by face and certainly vouch for his character. He wasn't some kind of vagabond theater hand. He was loyal, he said. Deeply committed to art. Plus, he added, he couldn't imagine a greater honor than "to take out the eighth wonder of the world."

Sarah said he was a darling. But she was hardly paying attention, spinning, her spirit being whisked away by the street parade.

Max let Nick lead the way, for the first time taking notice of the boy's slim hips and smooth shoulders.

Nick took them into Hsing's Laundry. A known regular, he guided them into the back room where the air clouded in thick smoke. Three couches lined the room. Only one was occupied, by a white couple. Middle-aged louts slouched with spread legs, and heads dropped against the back of the couch. Vacant eyes staring at the ceiling. A yellow light lit the room, cast from the soft glow of the opium lamps set on trays throughout the space. They were made of brass and set low. The side engravings of poppy plants slithered like ghostly shadows.

A young petite Chinese girl with firm posture greeted Nick. She motioned him and his guests to go behind a partition to a private room. Her face carried the seriousness of a craftsman with a newly mastered art. Once behind the divider, she looked at all three clients at once and motioned them to sit on the couch. Despite no obvious authoritative presence in the room, there was the eerie sensation that the girl herself was being watched. "Tell her we have our own," Max instructed Nick.

"A little unusual."

"We'll pay anyway."

Sarah sat in the middle. The couch springs gave lightly. Dust rose from the knotted wool upholstery, smelling of age. Max had Nick give the girl the canister. "For three, please," he instructed her in broken Cantonese.

The girl brought over a large bamboo pipe, ornate like a flute, sealed with ivory plugs at each end, with a wooden bowl set in brass near the top. She made two pills and dropped them into the bowl to cook over the lamp's rising blue flame. In a dutiful manner she knelt down reticently without eye contact and offered the first pipe to Sarah. A large puff of smoke leaked from the corners of Sarah's mouth. "Wow." She sighed, then laid her head back. The girl followed suit with Nick. When Max took his hit, he felt the smoke swallow deep down into his lungs, burning and searing. His head felt light, and for a moment his heart raced like he was coming home to Jesus. Then each of his muscles relaxed in descending order, from scalp to feet. He could feel the sinew and muscle expelling the tension, breathing out the daily cramping, and settling into pure relaxation. His face became very hot and glowed red. Then the warmth washed evenly through his entire body in one magnificent rush, vein by vein.

Twenty minutes later they did it again, and Hsing's Laundry on Mott Street became about the sweetest, most peaceful place on earth. For Max, a gangly boy reared back and forth between the North End of London and the seedy Reeperbahn of Hamburg, he had made it. He had endured taunts most of his life. Had had brutal chaps pinch his ass, then slug a fist across his jaw when he turned around. They said that's what happens to queers around here. At sixteen, his father had caught him bum high, mouth on a dick, and beat the shit out of his boy before tossing him out and reporting to the rest of the Klein family that the boy had run away and been lost at sea. He went to Paris. Mixed-up sad and crazy. Trying to toughen the outside to bury the inside. Dancing in the streets. Finally free from the crap he'd grown up with. That was ten years ago. Met Sarah. She needed someone who could organize. She hired him. He looked out for her. Did everything from read lines with her to pack her clothes to escort her lovers out in the middle of the night to brokering midnight performance deals to ensure that she could pay the next week's bills. He'd seen some crazy shit. But he was alive and happy. The wounds were healed. And now he sat a graceful bird perched on a couch in almighty America after negotiating $1,000 per performance plus 50 percent of the gross. That along with incidentals would bring in almost $4,000 per night on this golden American tour (as long as they didn't mess it up with some kind of foolishness like being bagged with illicit narcotics). He had finally landed. Safe. His hand resting on Nick's knee while remarkably still in adoration of Madame Bernhardt. Warts and all.

The Chinese girl came around again to check like a good waitress in midmeal. No more than sixteen, her abashed closed-mouth smile made her look twelve. Sweetness and innocence. Sarah smiled and thanked her. "I finally have relaxed for the first time in ages," she said. "Tell that to the sisters at le Grandchamps convent."

The Chinese girl nodded. She clearly had no command of the English language besides *thank you* or *no sir* or *you like*. Mostly she knew how to smile.

"You know before I came on this trip I went to Elsinore to visit Hamlet's tomb. I also went to Ophelia's Spring, and visited some of the castles."

Max interrupted her. "She doesn't know a word that you're saying, sweetheart. Nor does she really care, I'm sure."

"Oh shush, Molly." She turned her attention back to the girl, who stood respectfully. "I'd played those roles over and over again, and I wanted to see the actual history. Thought that maybe I would understand more about Hamlet. I even hoped that he would speak to me from his tomb." She started to giggle then erupted into a full-blown laugh that shook the couch.

The girl stood with the same staid smile, hands at her sides.

Max tried to interrupt, but Sarah stopped him with a wave of her hand. He sat back and listened to her voice, even in

English as pure as gold and silk, without a trace of opiate slur.

"Ophelia's Spring was an ordinary creek. Everything was ordinary. And what I learned was that my imagining of Hamlet's world was far more detailed than what I actually saw. I mean I could maybe give you a handful of bits about the way the plants grew around the grave. Or the architecture of Kronberg Castle. But now if I close my eyes and recite:

> O heart lose not thy nature;
> let not ever the soul of Nero enter this firm bosom.
> Let me be cruel, not unnatural.

I can smell the must of the castle. The fear that sweats off Hamlet, and the ruthlessness that shames Polonius. Odd-shaped stones and bricks mortar the gray walls, and the floor has a light cover of dust that dulls an otherwise ornate tile. It is cold. Joints ache. Cheeks are flushed. And the moisture hangs heavy in the air."

The girl stared, looking down at her feet once. For a moment she appeared nervous, as though still being observed. She scratched her nose, then looked up again to meet Sarah's eyes. And smiled.

Nick watched in fascination as he gripped Max's hand.

"Sometimes I get bored and start to distrust myself. I feel like a fraud, and I start to become like an accident victim trying to walk again. Where each step is lumbering and nothing is natural . . . I learned more about myself from that trip. My own eyes are liars. It's the well inside my head that knows the only truth."

The girl politely smiled in response to Sarah's laugh. She bowed graciously, then backed away, suddenly anxious.

"Please, one more," Sarah requested.

They sat for another hour without speaking. Max held on to Nick's hand the whole time, melting away, stripped to the vapor essence that was neither Max Klein nor homo nor rectifier nor confidant—just a solitary breath in the room.

When they finally left, Max said Nick could keep whatever was left over. He gave it to the girl as a tip.

They shared a taxi uptown. In the hallway of the Albermarle hotel, Nick and Max kissed furiously. Then Nick went into Sarah's room. An hour later he knocked on Max's door.

The next day the cast had rehearsed *L'Etrangère* at the Booth with more life than it had ever known. At the end of the day, standing backstage, Max hugged Sarah. He wept. "I'm sorry," he said between sobs. "I just haven't felt this happy before."

ON THE VENICE PIER, Sarah yawned. Still in Max's arms. "I am too tired to disagree," she said. "You will still look out for me, right? Never secrets or agendas."

Max released his hold. He took her hand and looked her in the eyes. They were sadder than he could remember, drawn back and worn. He squeezed her hand tighter. He never felt as desperate about protecting anybody as he felt for her. He would sit here all night and cradle her if she needed. He would make sure that nothing disrupted her career. She couldn't afford it financially and emotionally. He would make sure that she didn't smoke hop just to brighten her eyes and remember her smile. These were different times. The world was not so free and easy anymore. Judgment sat perched with a gavel that was

far heavier than it had ever been before. People were stronger.
Savvier. They were more vindictive. And the punishments more
severe. She didn't see that; in many respects she was too naive
to even understand the critical world surrounding her. But
she was not immune to its effects. She was wounded. Her hand
clasped against the bruise with no idea why she was struck. It
wasn't her world. She just lived there and performed for it.

"Can we go back to the hotel now, Max? I am tired."

He put his arm around her shoulder and guided her out of
the inlet. The length of the pier had become shadowed under a
drifting cloud. "First you need to stop by and tell Kinney that
the theater looks great. We don't want him to be concerned
about anything."

"But, Molly . . . I'm tired. And we still need to read through
the scene."

"This stop will only take a necessary minute."

"Always looking out for me."

Inside Kinney's office Sarah firmed her posture and spoke
confidently about the theater. Good acoustics. Nice stage. When
Kinney asked if she was sincere, she merely winked and said
in a breathy voice, *"Mais oui."* She was first and foremost an
actress. Max could always rely on that. When he was finally
assured of Kinney's satisfaction, Max announced that Sarah
needed her afternoon nap. Kinney said he would show her the
newspapers later. He smiled. He was proud. He thought she
should be too. They were defining a new history.

Sarah and Max left through the front door. The clouds
had passed. The pier was bright again. As he closed the door,
Max looked back to Kinney. The don of Venice pretended to
be relentlessly engaged in his papers.

Vince Baker's morning came too soon, despite the late hour at which he arose. His night had started around midnight at Willie's with a dame named Muriel who managed to stay one drink ahead of him until closing time. She was tall and brassy. Big hips that swelled from a tiny rib cage. Her hair could have been any color. Everything took on the same hue in the sepia cigar cloud that palled over the room. She laughed with a howl in the raucous moments, and pouted full mommy lips when the scene called for sympathy. By the end of the night Muriel was slumped unapologetically against the bar, her last bit of grace cupping a highball, eyes half closed.

He woke Muriel to tell her that he needed to go, he was late. She had a pinch of surprise in her eyes, only partially startled, though not so for the situation but for the realization that her prince had turned out to be just another member of the court. They recognized the disappointment in each other's eyes, and both smiled with the graciousness of a track bettor whose long shot pick didn't do better than show. Baker walked with her out the door. They shook hands. Forgot to say good-bye.

Waiting on his desk at the newsroom was a note from Graham Scott, saying that this morning's story warranted some discussion—as soon as Baker bothered to arrive. Baker sighed while he reached for the morning edition. Normally he would have scoured it front to back by now, discerning the paper's agenda and projecting where he might be heading for his next story. But with the morning slipping away he had not only failed to see the paper, he had also nearly forgotten to look at it. He kicked his feet up on his desk, straightening the periodical and ironing out the fold. There, front-page bottom left-hand corner, was a photo of Abbot Kinney on his pier. Stately and dignified. One hand tucked into his breast pocket while the other gestured with a punctuated but nonaccusatory forefinger. Below his byline, the cutline read "Kinney's Cultural Renaissance." His article began just as he had turned it in, describing Kinney true to form, giving a brief mention of his new Venice development and referring to him as a former tobacco man who had turned his energies and wealth toward promoting a cultural alternative to the ever-growing Los Angeles region. His only mention of Sarah Bernhardt that made the final cut in the article was a pro forma line that said that Bernhardt would be the first major act to perform at Venice, followed by a quote from Kinney that stated "she was having a rather splendid time enjoying this new view of California. And enjoying the fishing." The end. Baker didn't write about her mutilating the fish. Although he enjoyed her show from the pier, it was hardly the kind of thing he would bother with. Instead he chose to focus the ending on a recap of the League of Decency and the controversy that led into yesterday, closing with a comment by the bishop's mouthpiece, Dorothy O'Brien, that said something to the effect that Bernhardt was a public nuisance. An ending that never saw print.

Baker threw the *Herald* down and grabbed for the competing editions of the *Record*, *Evening Express*, and *Examiner*. Same shit. All the other articles read like a group of conspiring college freshman plagiarizing the same primary source, only inverting a word or phrase in hoodwinked originality. They all wrote about the incident from the pier as if it were the only news in the world. Detailing the drama and theatrics, clearly not intrigued nor willing to understand, approaching it only as sensational drivel to rile the readership. The *Register* was the only paper to offer any deeper suggestion of Bernhardt's exile. But even still, its focus was a page-eight picture of her on the dock next to Kinney, with the caption reading "The French stage star enjoys the California sun." Like it was part of the goddamned weather forecast. "Sonabitch," he said to himself.

Following a summons, he marched back to Graham Scott's office, brushing past Barb, the secretary, who organized her papers conspicuously while watching him from the corner of her eye.

His feet felt as if they were pounding the floor and rocking the entire building. He knew that his face was turning red, paling the pouched bags beneath his eyes. He could really use a smoke about now. He repeatedly dried his sweaty hands against his slacks, leaving streaked finger stains.

Graham Scott rolled his eyes up to greet his visitor. His cheek was cupped in his hand as he studied a pile of feature stories being considered for Sunday's paper. His eyes were tired and glassy but not unusually so. They always had a watery jaundiced quality about them. He didn't move when Baker entered his office. Still kept the full weight of his head propped on his right elbow. He had been in the business almost since it first became a business. He had done his time on the streets before settling into his career as a managing editor. There was not much that he hadn't seen, but still he never did get that one story to hang his hat on. In his day he had covered it all, from politics to crime, all of it being relevant to the times, but he had never managed to capture a defining story like so many of his colleagues had. He saw himself as a good defensive second baseman who made the plays day in and day out but was never the hero of the game. But the guy knew this town.

He had really hit his stride when he moved to the editorial side. He had a knack for organization and, perhaps most importantly, the unique grace to balance between the needs of his reporters and the demands from the upstairs Mahogany Row boys. That was why he liked Vince Baker. With his work everybody looked good.

Baker didn't bother to announce himself. "You called?" he said.

Scott didn't even need to point to the paper. "Why this shit when there was a real story?"

"If there is any real story in this nonsense, then the boycott is it."

Scott shook his head. "Come on, Vince."

"Politics. Manipulation. Greed. All the basic ingredients for cooking up any story."

Scott straightened up then leaned back in his chair, crossing his arms over a recently acquired potbelly. "One of the most famous stage actresses smothers a fish over her face, and that's nothing? *Politics. Manipulation. Greed.* When the other three idiot papers here report on it, doesn't that give you a sense of its newsworthiness? Everybody in this town is talking about Sarah-on-the-Pier except for the ignoramuses who subscribe to our paper. Why? Because they don't know about it. From now on, give me the stories as they happen. If something real comes up again about the boycott, then by all means give it to me. But it appears that the story is elsewhere."

Baker sucked in a deep inhalation. The burst of anger had exhausted him, it withdrew the last bit of stamina he had from only fours hours' worth of sleep. He sat down, leaning forward on Scott's desk. "Please just take me off the story altogether. Give me something that matters."

"Vince." Scott leaned forward paternally, his old-man breath suggesting a vintage and proof more high-falutin' than what was being served at Willie's last night. "Take a look at all the other dailies. This matters . . . You're on the assignment until she leaves town."

"Why not Seabright? That's his circle."

"Because I don't want to get scooped again. I want the story no one else has—which I suppose I got this time. From now on, just give me your usual. That's all I am asking for."

Baker left Scott's office with half the stride he came in with. *Fuck me*, he thought to himself. He just needed to rest. Have a smoke and a sleep. Forget about things for a while. Maybe a trip down to Willie's later would do him good. See if Muriel is still at the bar. Figure out how to build a house without the foundation.

He sat down at his desk and laid his head on a stack of notes, wishing he had never awoken Muriel.

SARAH LAY ACROSS THE BED in her room at the King George with the afternoon edition of the *Register* spread at her side. Black smudges from the tips of her fingers streaked the linen sheet like ashen snakes. The picture looked terrible. Caught her back, with that imbecile Kinney obviously intent on trying to block off the cameras. It could have been anybody sitting on that pier. She felt disgraced. As per usual these days, nobody talked about art in this article. There wasn't a single mention of the play, or even a tidbit to suggest the notion that Dumas *fils* had written *La Dame aux Camélias* especially for her. Instead it focused on her at the pier as though she was merely engaged in the antics of her history. Clearly the reporter wanted nothing other than to witness the return of the younger Sarah. The only other focal point was on Abbot Kinney pissing a line across the beach and daring only the enlightened to cross it.

There was no talk of artistry. How she had made the commitment to growing her craft when she could have easily retreated and relied on her celebrity. Nothing critical and worthy about how a sixty-one-year-old woman had renovated the signature role of her youth in *La Dame aux Camélias* into a near-perfect hallmark for aging women (if she could only nail down that ending). As the visage of youth clearly receded, Sarah had managed to transform that wayward sixteen-year-old girl into someone who defied age. In her younger days Sarah had enveloped the role with her own girlish exuberance, swift movements and coy expressions, delivering sardonic lines between shallow breaths as though a head full of ideas would explode like an un-tined baked potato. She had embodied the very essence of untamed youth. Girlish energy that sailed off the skin without depth, and the only time the heart was truly accessed was when it had been unsuspectingly fractured, leaving little room not for analysis or reflection, but rather for the buoyant reaction of passion and lust. But at age sixty-one, she had revived her character beyond the reactive and into the mindful. As she drifted off into sleep she had thought to herself the other night that she was really no longer playing Marguerite Gautier, but that she was now playing Marguerite's soul. Onstage, her delivery was slow and deliberate, as though she had taken each line and wrapped it in silk, then let it glow under the moonlight. She considered. Contemplated. She transformed reactions into thoughtful analysis. She let go of Marguerite's body and only took her eyes. All anybody in that audience needed to do was to look deep into her gaze for one moment, and then they could know Marguerite Gautier. They would know her pain. Her confusion. Her sorrow. Marguerite Gautier was no longer a sixteen-year-old who would die at twenty embittered by the disconnection between love, survival, and success. She was the embodiment of mature human emotion. And maybe that was where the problem lay with the final scene. She did not know how to concede that emotion to something beyond her—like disease. It was too wrapped up in itself, layer upon layer, to fall prey to any outside influences. She had always played Marguerite from the perspective that the disease was some incarnation that had come to battle for the rights of Marguerite's soul—of course calling into question the idea of "right" and "pure." But now she started to wonder if the disease was nothing more than a haphazard bump of luck. Sure, Marguerite had chosen a life that was looked down upon by others, but not all kept women are cut down by disease as a divine act of retribution, just as they are not all given to finding true love. Maybe that is what was troubling Sarah so much. She couldn't find a connection between the virus and the life.

Sarah rolled to her side, again looking at the paper. *Merde.* She swatted it off the bed, where the pages fluttered down to the short teal rug. She told herself to remind Max that she didn't want to see the papers anymore.

The opium was wearing off. The emptiness settling in. An overwhelming sadness that was not solely tied to her mental state but was instead a pathos that embodied every fiber of her body. Her thighs felt bad. Her skin anguished. Her ribs bereaving. She was thankful to be lying down now, because next the craving would take over, driving and commanding her to do anything she could to smolder the poignancy, which meant usually another hit of opium or a long dreary sleep. It was that exact moment of indecision where it seemed that everything that haunted her took place. The moment when the sadness became too much to bear. Where she lifted her skirt and showed her bare legs to a world too intrigued to turn their heads, yet too paralyzed to do anything except abandon her in Christian fear. Maybe she should have been more private over the years. Perhaps those moments of public display would not have been the executioner to her career. People probably wouldn't have assigned so much meaning to the roles she had been playing, instead they would have watched them for the beauty and artistry. But it wasn't just about opium. She had lived her whole life flirting with those moments of sadness. The drugs only gave a false sense of medication when it became too much to handle, then served to heighten the feeling when the numbing wore off. She tried to tell Max that a thousand times. In fact, they had just had the conversation two weeks ago on a train leaving Chicago. But Max didn't seem able to understand. Even when she had said that she lived her whole life with these feelings. Even in cushioned seats, face-to-face in a private car, not two feet from the intense heat burning off her skin was he able to see beyond the effects and control of narcotics. He loved her that much.

Maybe this really should be her farewell tour of America. That was something she and Max had cooked up one night in Paris to add some drama to the tour, and more importantly to add some revenue. They laughed about the Americans' craving for establishing some form of history, and that they would always gladly buy it at top dollar. The Divine Sarah Bernhardt's last tour of America. The last show in Chicago. The last performance in New York. In Los Angeles. Where each farewell was a moment of history, and every fully paying audience member a part of that history. They laughed when they discussed the idea. Giggled in delight at their shrewdness, with the private duplicity of children outwitting their parents. But maybe it wasn't so clever anymore. How quickly the hypochondriac becomes the diseased, the punch line its own joke. She could end it now silently. Take the last bouquet of roses thrown to her feet, hold them up beside her head, sweet perfume overpowering the bitter sweat of performance, smile coyly to the standing crowd, squint her eyes in the footlights and graciously bow to the auditorium center-right-left-center, gesturing an offer of the roses back to the admirers, and step away slowly off the stage into the maze of ropes and darting stagehands and massaging sycophants. She wouldn't say good-bye. Treat it as just another night. Only there would be no tomorrow. Strike the stage. Bury the scripts in a trunk. Cancel the train tickets. A slow boat back to France. Retiring to the fluff of her bed, where she would run her thin fingers along her parsed and calloused heels, digging her nails deeply into the leathery skin, amazed that she feels no pain, until she finally reaches over and grabs the skin cream and massages it into her heels, thinking about how great it is to not be an actor anymore. She could give it up.

Sarah dangled her arm off the bed and swatted at the newspaper. Max was due soon. And she had not changed out of her nightgown yet. The entire walk back from Kinney's office he had implored her to rest, sleep to take the edge off of what he had described as a "frightful yet manageable bump in the arse." Then a good dinner would help settle things. A gastronomic cure can always heal the ills of the mind. "Anything other than the King George," she had said.

"Kinney spoke highly of it. He said your recommendation would back him up."

"Anything other than the King George."

Max had assured her that he would find a different restaurant. She could tell by the deliberate pauses between words and the evenly stressed syllables that he assumed her doped beyond comprehension. Still he had been gentle and nonplacating. She allowed him his concern. She didn't protest with annoyance or insult. She had just looked down, smiling at the misted walkway and repeated, "Anything other than the King George."

Now she hoped that he didn't pick anything too nice. An advantage to eating in the United States was that one did not always have to dine. No meals where course upon course was delivered throughout the evening. The European edict of civility and formality was eschewed in the American restaurant. You could eat because you were simply hungry. Any time of day. Sit down and read the menu and order to your heart's delight. In America you can get "a bite." She looked forward to that on all her tours. But of course most people wanted to entertain her at the finer restaurants that replicated the European experience, either run by displaced emigrants or born-and-bred citizens bored with their American-ness. Tonight she wanted simplicity. She wanted to forget the doting and camaraderie and deference. She wanted to figure out how she could leave all this behind. Roll up her blouse sleeves, put her bare elbows to the table, and lean forward with a prejudice for honesty. She didn't want to just blurt out a statement that seemed derivative of thoughtless passion, and watch Max's face drop before he settled into a logic marathon that eventually converted her out of nothing else other than pure boredom

and wear. Not this time. Now she wanted an understanding
built. Even if nothing changed. If she ended up doing the
same thing until she was one hundred and one years old, at
least there would be an understanding of why she decided to
continue. And Max probably wouldn't get it. He would likely do
one of his Molly gestures, swatting his hands around, rolling
his eyes and pursing his lips. (Max Klein would have made
a hell of an actor, because he understood the importance of
gestures and their use in making the finer points. She told him
that often. He never listened.) But she knew this time that he
would be absolutely mad with fear, and his arms would fly in
a pedestrian rage. She would tell him not to worry. They could
still continue on. There is more to life than acting. It's just
one thing. They could run a hospital. She had done it before.
She had put acting aside during the Franco-Prussian war and
started a military hospital at the Odéon. The establishment and
the reporters all had had a good laugh about it. Wrote stories
about the dainty little stage star traveling to the Ministry of
War and requesting the authority to open a military hospital.
Some thought it was cute. Others a show of patriotism that
would last as long as the next curtain's rising. But months and
months went by. She held the hands of the infirm. Patted cold
towels on feverish foreheads. Sought food for the wounded
brave. Met the ambulances at the front. Carried stretchers to
the basement when Paris was bombarded. And the whole time
she made sure the flag always flew, all the way through the
armistice being signed. There was nothing darling or adorable
about what she had done. It was sweat. It was blood. And
acting had been the furthest thing from her consciousness
until the war had ended. The Divine Sarah had walked offstage
and been hung on the costume rack as the stage was struck,

waiting until the marquee shone again, while the real Sarah
(or was it Henriette-Rosine?) held her breath in constant fear,
trying to steady her hands and voice in the name of calm and
comfort. There is more than just the theater out there, Molly.
She would tell him that. More than just the stage life. All kinds
of roles to play. Even for a Molly House boy trying to belong.

Sarah stared up at the ceiling, admiring the smooth plaster.
A hotel room new enough that there were not even cracks yet.
The ceiling reached higher than she had imagined. Almost
as arching as the prayer room had been at the Grandchamps
convent where the budding novices were corralled daily, taken
from being giggling squeaky girls and transformed into silent,
respectful conduits of God's word. They would be marched in
single file out of the butter-lit fields and placed an arm's length
apart on dark wooden pews where candle shadows often made
strange and ghostly images. Then they would kneel. Forget the
girl next to them. This was just about you and God, until there
was no you. The real weakness, the true temptation for most of
the girls, was not to laugh. Something about the abject silence
and the forbiddingness of the room tempted hysterics. The
trick was not to look at your neighbor. If you could resist eye
contact, you would soon be absorbed into the wholeness of God.
But if you laughed, you would be absorbed into the Mother
Superior's ire, which usually concluded with a strap across
the hand, followed by an excruciatingly long silence from her
that might last through two meals. When the pressure became
too great, Sarah's trick was to pinch her leg. She would move
her hand up her dress until it touched her inner thigh, then
she would squeeze a tuft of skin until the urge to laugh had
subsided. The privacy of her thighs covered the shame of black
bruises. Sometimes she left her hand there. In the cavern of

piousness, where all was sacred and guarded by unseen powers, the softness of her skin left her reassured that her corporeal body was connected to God's comfort. She knew if she were ever caught that the Mother Superior would think her dirty, and though she might not actually say it aloud, would assume that this was the result of the Jewish blood that had flowed down through Sarah's grandmother. They were a dirty people who could never know the cleanliness of truly loving God. They left Christ to be killed on that cross and never washed their hands again. Mother Superior as much as said that once to Sarah, hoping to undermine Sarah's unspoken ancestry. Sarah had nodded politely, thinking to herself that if there wasn't that Christ hanging off the cross, what would there be left for the church to talk about? Still the fear of being caught never stopped Sarah's hand. She secreted her fingers to her thigh with every prayer. And she never once felt dirty. Nor afraid. Nor was there anything sexual about it. She still spoke her prayers. But felt a little more whole. More connected to herself.

As she remembered, she found her hand resting on the same spot on her thigh where it lay fifty years ago. The skin no longer held the smoothness. It had loosened, leaving more sinew and bone for the touch. Her poor thigh. Too many uncaring hands that could never pause long enough to feel the comfort and solace had touched it. It had merely become part of the route where fumbling fingers carelessly floundered in search of greater pleasures. Perhaps she had started to believe that as well. She never stopped those hands. Never insisted on a pause to luxuriate in the comfort. Instead she had bought into the myth of male pleasure, that there were only three parts of a woman's body that brought satisfaction, and the inner thigh was not one of them. She stopped questioning. And though she couldn't really recall any specific moment—maybe it was all as part of a gradual fade—she had nearly forgotten the calming and connectedness brought to her by that part of her body. A place where no man's calloused hand should have ever touched anyhow.

There was a knock on the door. "One moment, Molly," she answered, recognizing the waltzing percussion of his announcement. She didn't want to move, at least not for another moment. She didn't want to think about acting. About business. About renegade Catholic causes. She just wanted to be Henriette-Rosine back in the convent again, surrounded by silence and wholeness. Her hand on her thigh, feeling the stillness of her breath, the minuscule sounds of knees shifting and noses sniffling, where solace was the only success. Washing herself of all those who had touched her and tried to make her peace their peace. Just being still again. And feeling her own feelings.

Max's knock turned impatient.

She forced herself up from the bed. Her head felt light. She could feel the weight of blood pushing to her feet. She stepped over the newspaper, one more time looking at that useless page-eight picture. She put her heel right over the smudged image of her back and scattered the newspaper under the bed with a series of short kicks, like a dog trying to cover up his shit. She patted the side of her hair into place. Ran her fingers like a comb through the back, snagging on a small tangle that she impatiently crooked with her index finger and broke. She looked tired. She knew it. Max would assume it was the aftermath of the opium. It was impossible for him to just see her as tired. She knew that, too. In fact, how he saw her was probably her fault. She had cultivated and appropriated all the details of the actress Sarah.

He was smiling when she opened the door. The light caught his hazel irises just enough to bring out the green. He looked at her in her gown. Then back to the mussed bed with the edges of newspaper peering out from underneath. "Good gracious," he said. "I figured you would be ready by now."

"Did we set a time?"

"About ten years ago."

She laughed. "We manage everything, don't we?"

"To the last detail."

Max walked into the room, slipping between her and the door. He sat down at the blond desk placed directly across from the matching headboard, the dented pillows reflecting in its mirror.

She closed the door, stood still for a moment, and then sat down at the edge of the bed. She ran her hands over her cheeks, feeling the tenderness of her skin. "We are not going to the King George, are we?"

"There is a driver downstairs waiting to take us to a restaurant downtown that the concierge recommended."

"I need quiet."

"Supposedly it is."

"That is my one request."

"Only one?"

"And no Abbot Kinney."

"You think that I would do that to either of us?" He looked at her in the mirror with a slight smile. "Besides, that is two requests, and we need to go. The car is waiting."

"If you want me to change clothes, then stop looking at me. You think this is the Moulin Rouge? No free show here, Molly."

"Frankly, I would rather have pitchforks in my eye than be caught unawares by a female breast."

"Then look the other way, or go ask your friend Abbot Kinney for a pitchfork."

"I would certainly take a pitchfork in the eyes before having to set sight on that pretense."

She rose from the bed and stepped behind Max, looking away from her reflection in the mirror. She placed her hands on his shoulders and squeezed tenderly. "I love my Molly. I truly do. But I need you to help me through how I see Marguerite."

"We will get through this," he said. "We get through it all."

She squeezed his shoulders again. "You know that I love you, don't you?"

He reached back and took her hands. His grip was confident. His hands warm and manicured. "You know Marguerite better than you know yourself." He laughed. "Again, you find yourself distracted by loudmouth fanatics that are angry at their God for putting them in a world they detest. The only way they can maintain their faith is to find someone else to blame. There is no justice here. Only ignorance. And we are professionals at dealing with ignorance, we have managed it with every American tour . . . And, yes, I do know how much you love me. I tell myself every day."

She didn't move her hands. She wished he could hold them forever. She swallowed and fought back a tear. Her eyes could have exploded. "All right then," she said, wanting to tell him that yes they may have been through this time after time on their American tours, but now she was wearied by it, and it suddenly felt like anything but routine, and even at that this chaos had nothing to do with not being able to see Marguerite anymore. She loosened her grip and gave Max a pat on the shoulders that seemed suddenly chummy. "You sit tight, dear.

I'll change in the bathroom. Don't want pitchforks in your eyes."

"You don't have to—"

"The beige blouse, or the puritanical white?" She pointed to the open closet.

"Sarah, I can wait outside."

"Beige or white?"

"White. But don't wear puritanical white. Wear angelic white."

"Better for the Catholics, I suppose."

"They'll see your shoulder blades as wings."

"And you'll be my guardian angel."

"Can an angel have a penis?"

"If they can have wings, I don't see why not."

"Well." Max smiled. "We'll just have to ask Bishop What's-His-Name when we see him. Penises and wings . . . What's the answer, Mr. Bishop? . . . Penises and wings. Penises and wings. How Greek of us."

"My Molly." Sarah walked into the bathroom despite Max's final protests. The lavatory had a sterile sheen. The floor laid out in glossy black and white tiles positioned as connecting diamonds. The freestanding porcelain sink blended into the floor, and behind a milky bath curtain the tile pattern repeated itself in an ivy climb up the wall before stopping abruptly at the plaster. She draped her clothes over the curtain rod and sat down on the toilet. The seat, crisp from the partially open window, almost stung her bare bottom. The trickling of pee into the water was almost silent. And through the window shone only a slip of natural light, the rest clouded and blurred through the leafy pattern of the beveled glass. Almost as artificial and contrived as sunrise appearing through the glass panes on the set of Marguerite's traveling 9, rue d'Antin flat. Swear to god, if it weren't for the crack of natural light Sarah wouldn't know the difference between the stage and reality.

AL LEVY'S ON THIRD AND MAIN was a trendy type of restaurant that had made oyster cocktails highbrow, just the type where a concierge would undoubtedly send a guest. It reeked of kickbacks and questionable funding, but where an assumed pact was made with the patrons to become coconspirators in the illusion of East Coast sophistication. The lighting was sparkly silver, set by a row of Italian imported chandeliers that hung in two straight lines along the almost impossible length of the vaulted ceilings. Each tinsel of glass was no doubt cleaned daily by an underpaid Mexican duped into believing that he had been immaculately chosen to apprentice for a dignified trade critical to keeping the American dream moving—making sure the diamonds sparkled. A grand elegant staircase rose from the center of the dining floor, with mahogany steps at least eight feet in length, made royal by a red woolen runner that draped the middle, balanced by a matching banister with carved lions' heads at both top and bottom. The ascent up the stairs led to the balcony, and in the balcony was the bar, where a pianist in tails intermingled Mozart and Joplin.

Vince Baker sat at the end of the bar. Gone upscale for an evening. Maybe half a chance at meeting a sophisticated puss who would be seduced by his combination of rough edges and power. No promises. No odds. No hard feelings if he walked away alone. As with most nights he was content with avoiding his lonely box of an apartment, which, despite being new and in a more desirable location, felt just as empty and terrifying

as every other place where he had lived. The only times he
ever felt a connection to the outside world from his quarters
were the occasions when the woman four times his age in
the apartment across the street would stare vacantly out the
window behind a single candle, a sad expression, wearing only
a gigantic bra that looked more akin to a Visigoth's armor. He
held his place quietly at the end of the bar, wearing a rumpled
dress coat pulled from a pile in his closet (his most suitable
attire), looking out over the dining room at the patrons in
their quest for Los Angeles culture. He'd give it twenty minutes
or three more drinks, whichever came first, and then it was
the next cab down to Willie's for a nightcap and a shot at the
last-chance dolls.

He hadn't caught any rest at all today. Hadn't done much
of anything other than contribute to a follow-up on some City
Hall scandal by getting a quote from a chirpy clerk hoping to
make his mark through squawking. Baker probably wouldn't
even get a credit on the byline for that, but who really cared.
He had spent the better part of the day trying to sniff out
something good, a hot tip on some action that was going down,
anything that he could take back to Scott to get him off the
Bernhardt story.

By his third rusty nail he was beginning to consider the idea
of just quitting. He lit up another cigarette, feeling the breeze
of cool smoke calm his chest.

By the fourth rusty nail he kept a hawkish vigilance over
the room.

He moved seats until he was tucked into the corner,
camouflaged by a potted palm tree and the jacked-up hood of
the grand piano. His own voyeur's nest, where he could watch
up close without being seen, not as a reporter, but as a person

fascinated by the quirks of his own species. Still he took care to keep himself hidden. This was the kind of place where the power brokers that he covered would seek refuge. They loved joints like this; made them feel like the wild Spanish-American west had been made submissive through opulent grace. Baker scooted his stool deeper into the corner. He didn't want any of these somebodys to look up from their sparkling tables, champagne toasts in hand, and see him looking down on them, mistaking him for one of those F. T. Seabright types, covertly eavesdropping to get their story and *make news*.

Max held the grand door of Al Levy's for Sarah. She graced in, immediately intrigued by the restaurant's dark elegance yet disappointed by the obviousness of its idea, and that it lacked the informality that she had been hoping for. It was masterfully contrived, designed with the same artisanship of a master set builder, but still she felt the thinness of the walls, like a stretched canvas framed with boards, with the scene painted on the facing sides. It would not take more than a convergence of errant sneezes to accidentally blow the whole place down. It was as though she had entered stage left into a generic Europe from backstage Los Angeles.

She and Max waited at the door near the host's podium. She had eschewed the idea of wearing a blouse but did stick with the idea of white in the form of a long, elegant dress whose hem gracefully dragged the floor. The material, thin batiste cotton (a fabric chosen for most of her California wardrobe, all tailored by Laferriére), flowed with a ghostly elegance. She looked to be in motion even when standing still. The greeting area was dark, lit only by two candelabras, clearly affected to further the drama of walking into the sparkling dining room. To an unsuspecting diner who happened to glance toward the front entrance, Sarah must have looked like a passing apparition in that hollow.

"Are you sure about this, Molly?" she asked, taking a short step backward.

"What I know is that the concierge recommended it." He leaned into the empty host's stand and drummed his finger against the hard wood.

"Maybe that's it. It seems like a place that people think we would like."

Max shook his head. He had been through this too many times to remember. Her first instinct was always to find the faults. Once she could identify everything wrong or suspect about where they were, then she could settle in to enjoy herself. "We don't have to stay," he said in an almost rehearsed fashion.

"Maybe if we could just be seated."

"I don't see the host."

"Being seated would make it better."

Max looked out into the dining room for someone who could assist them to their table.

"We have a reservation for sure?" Sarah asked.

"Concierge said he made it."

"And you tipped him, I assume. You know they expect that here, don't you?"

"Sarah, please."

She threw her arms around his neck, adopting the role of the old lush. "Oh Molly," she whispered, childlike. "Relax your ass cheeks. If we could just sit down is all that I'm saying. I'm so fatigued."

They waited for five impossible minutes. Max began shifting foot to foot while his breathing hardened. It was difficult to know whether he was truly annoyed with the lack of service, or if he was anticipating his employer's reaction.

Sarah finally fulfilled Max's prophecy. "This seems an unusual amount of time to wait," she said.

"I am doing my best."

"The rest of our crew will reach Los Angeles before we get a table."

"Sarah."

"I am only joking, Molly. Please. Personal is not becoming on you . . . Maybe the host is upstairs by the bar. Perhaps we should check."

"Maybe," Max said, then suggested that Sarah should wait in the foyer in case the host did in fact arrive. He would go upstairs and check around. But she insisted on going with him, that she didn't want to be left alone. All it would take would be one crazy Catholic to notice her, and then Sarah wasn't sure that she could be responsible for how she might handle the situation.

They made a child's pact. They would walk halfway up the stairs and then stop. Sarah would look up. Max would look down. If there was not a host to greet them by that point then they would descend the stairs, head straight out the door into a waiting cab with a directive to get to the nearest diner.

By the second step Sarah knew that she had been seen. There is a certain shift in the dynamic of the room whenever someone has made her—a pocket of silence followed by a downshift in volume, throwing off the balance of the room. Then it starts to spread. Sometimes a cancer. Sometimes dominoes. Until the entire space has adopted a new personality fueled by fascination and intrigue. It is at that precise moment, the one where the last voice has hushed, and a temporary silence stands, that she always knows when she has diseased the entire room, infected everyone there with her presence until they are consumed by her. On some level it does not really affect her, because it is intrinsic to her being; at the very least, it is the oxygen that keeps the being of Sarah Bernhardt the Stage Star breathing. Her dirty little secret is that the rest of the world doesn't know how critical they are to keeping that Sarah Bernhardt alive. The moment when that room doesn't take notice is the moment when Sarah Bernhardt wilts and withers away.

At the agreed upon halfway point, Sarah and Max stopped. She felt reinvigorated. Puffed with life. Her veins pure and free from the opium. She didn't acknowledge the spectators. That was part of the game. The distance was the fascination. She thought about her agenda to quit that she had concocted while back at the hotel, and smiled to herself. In a million years, Max would never believe her if she was to turn to him and say that she wanted out of the business. He would probably give her one of those Molly kisses, stretching on his tiptoes for no real reason and grasping both her shoulders while gracing her cheek with stiff lips. He would be right. Sort of. There were two things she did refuse to do: fade away or be shoved away.

Sarah looked up at the bar, letting her gaze follow the piano's melodic breeze along an empty dance floor big enough for two, then over to the bar where a slouch-shouldered bartender in a false black vest and white bow tie made time with a resentful cocktail waitress. Otherwise she didn't see anybody else up there, least of all the gentleman host. "And do you see anything?" she asked Max.

"Not even an empty table."

"We must remember to ask that concierge for your tip back."

They turned in choreographed precision. Max took her arm as a gentleman escort, and they descended the stairs as the genuine article, misplaced in this faux proscenium summer stock one-act of a restaurant. Shoulders back. Chins arched slightly. Eyes above the crowd. "I really did just feel like having a *croque monsieur*," she whispered, frowning in mock royalty to ensure a sense of mystery for all watchful eyes.

"The closest they have in America is a grilled cheese sandwich."

"That will do."

They walked down to the main floor and through the foyer without acknowledging or honoring any part of the surroundings. They didn't even notice the sound of the potted palm falling over upstairs. Or the spray of coins hastily tossed on the bar. Nor the awkward stumbling behind them on the stairs they had just left. Or even the slamming door of the cab behind them as Vince Baker directed the driver to "catch that cab."

MOST REPORTERS only get one chance. They get a single shot to pose their questions and establish their rapport. Unpreparedness. Boredom. Ignorance. Aloofness. Any combination of these integers will not only kill a story, but will also kill a reputation. There are no apologies. No second chances. Editors lose faith. The cubs on the dog watch start picking up the assignments, and you spend most of your days looking for some kind of dope that will lead you into the good fortune of a story that will reestablish your credibility on the street and in the newsroom. The bottom line, the lesson: Be prepared. Otherwise the business will eat you alive from the inside out.

VINCE BAKER HADN'T CONSIDERED IT irony but rather coincidence that Bernhardt's cab turned down Broadway and stopped in front of Ralph's—just around the corner from the Cathedral of our Lady of Angels—the very diner where he had drafted the beginning of the League of Decency boycott piece. He told the driver to keep the motor running as he watched Bernhardt get out of her car. She stood on the curb, looking into the Ralph's window while her slightly younger companion fumbled through his wallet, no doubt calculating the worth of his bills and exchanging the rates in his head. It was clear to Baker that Bernhardt's escort served in a professional capacity. He had a look of servitude in his posture. Confident and sure of himself. Poised to accommodate her in a way that only a smitten man who rarely saw night except for outside his window would behave given his one shot with a beautiful woman. But this man was no smitten agoraphobic. He stood a head taller than his mistress did, with a jacket cut so splendidly to his physique that neither he nor the jacket could be from anywhere else but the most sophisticated metropolises of Europe. His hair was dark, combed back slick and dapper. And he moved with a sophistication that seemed to transcend grace to the degree that Baker immediately pegged the man as being as queer as any of the swishy downtown types. Bernhardt and her escort were obviously familiar with each other. It was clear through the comforts of their smiles and their relaxed shoulders. They touched each other like it was common, unlike the consciously perpetrated brushing of potential lovers. Baker watched the man hold the door for her as she walked into that greasy dive with the same elegance and sophistication that she had just conferred on Al Levy's.

They disappeared into the back (though they were certainly not seeking an out-of-the-way table for clandestine purposes, rather from celebrity habit). Once their cab drove off, the street scene in front of Ralph's looked as lonely and desolate as the rest of the post-nine-o'clock downtown, where only a few windows were made alive by sickly yellow bulbs, and a wind that didn't seem to be there in daylight wound the streets like a scrounging snake kicking up stray sheets of paper that whipped through two or three violent somersaults before settling somewhere else up the sidewalk; where the scraping of trash and a whistling wind that was paradoxically silent were the only sounds other than that of a bum's cough or sneeze that echoed through the concrete canyon in such randomly acute angles that it was nearly impossible to pinpoint its origin; and where the purity of a desolate temperate night smelled both pungent and fragrant.

The cabbie said, "I don't meant to . . ." He looked straight ahead. Didn't bother to crane his neck.

Baker was still staring out his window. The rumbling of the cab vibrated his hands. "Don't mean to what?"

"You know."

"I'm not sure I do."

The cabbie paused. Then spoke as though he had carefully chosen his next word. "Meddle." His pronunciation divided the word by its two syllables.

"Meddle?"

"You know, get involved. Tell you what to do."

"I know the meaning of the word."

"Then why ask?"

"I didn't mean to imply that I didn't know the word *meddle*. It was more of what you meant by it." Jesus, his head was too bloated by scotch for this. And just the realization of that sent a fierce wave of nausea tiding up his throat.

"You know," the cabbie said, "the Chinese do crazy things in this kind of situation. I lived up in San Francisco—let's just say that I'm glad that I got out before the quake. But I know the Chinese. I know the crazy things they will do."

Baker was barely listening.

"They're very private people, they are. Very private."

"Who is that?" Baker gave partial attention.

"The Chinese. The Chinese is who I'm talking about. They are private people."

"What about them?"

"I'm just saying that they are private people. Chinese handle things their own ways."

"Well, thanks for telling me that." Baker needed to decide what to do. He had Bernhardt back at the vicinity of his crime. Every reporter on the police beat knows that that is the first place the cops go in a manhunt—back to the scene of the crime. Some think it is to relive the power and the glory, others think it is to try to make peace with the violence. For Baker it could have been either. It didn't matter. His assignment was sitting in the exact chair where he had sorted his notes from the bishop's interview. They wouldn't have to turn up the wattage of the electric lamp to get him to spill his guts. He'd cop to it. Rat himself out. He was there. Part of the plan. An accomplice. And that's murder by the legal definition.

"See, a Chinese guy in your situation . . ."

Jesus Christ, enough about the Chinese.

". . . He wouldn't do what you're doing. He would just off her in their home, then bury her out back. Whole little private Chinese community would know, but they wouldn't care. They'd say she had it coming. Honor. Wouldn't cry a tear for her. Husband would have the right to keep his honor. That's how they work. Honor and privacy. That's the Chinese for you."

"You think she's my wife? That's not my wife. She's double my age. She would be my mother, if anything." He was irritated that he found himself justifying his position to someone who was ultimately going to charge him when all was said and done.

"I told you I don't want to meddle."

"She's just someone who I've been trying to catch up with."

"You a private dick for somebody else?"

"It's not like that."

"If you say so . . . So there she is. Should I turn off the meter now?"

Baker couldn't go through with it. It wasn't that he was chicken shit, or even that he was too inebriated to steady his thoughts, it was that he wasn't ready. He had his subject. He had his chance to get her, turn in a story, and get Scott off his back. But he didn't have his angle. If he went in now the very least that he might get out with was some puff piece that would sadly chart a second-rate comparison to Seabright, something that would slaughter his credibility on the news beat (and that stuff will dog you the rest of your life). He closed his eyes for a moment, heavy and tired from the weight of the alcohol. In his mind he saw the Phoenix, Arizona, that he had grown up in. Small streets with low roofs. The intense heat thundering down. Tall brown mountains surrounding the valley, cutting a jagged edge across the horizon. A city of five thousand people who were all afraid to cross over Baltimore Street, terrified by the thought of open desert and vengeful Navajos. To a young man dreaming of escaping the livery stables and ostrich farms of Grand Avenue, the bright splashing orange sunsets seemed like they took place in some land greater and more powerful, whose color was not a gift but an accidental overflow pouring down the mountains. It took twenty years of dreaming to get across those mountains. Twenty years to find the center of the sunset. And he still didn't know which way to turn.

"Let's go," Baker said. "Drive."

"Sure?"

"I said, let's go . . . And try to avoid Second. I don't want to go by the cathedral there."

The cabbie released the brake. "Where to then?"

"Take me down by C. C. Brown's. You know it?"

Cabbie just nodded and drove, like it was all inside code.

Baker looked back at Ralph's. Couldn't see a goddamned thing. He had to trust his instincts and hope that he hadn't let one get away.

CHAPTER FOUR
May 16, 1906

THE dilemma for insomniacs is distinguishing the line between night and morning. The moment when Sarah gives up all hope of sleeping, driven by the rationale that it is morning anyway, and the promise of night has now been completely abandoned. She checked her clock to see a painful reading of 4:57 A.M. Partway into five o'clock meant usually giving in to the morning, forgetting about rest altogether, drawing a bath, and opening a curtain and letting the dusty little portents of the day filter in. But the three minutes before five were just enough to abuse the system, pitting a sleep deprivation that begged for mercy against an incarcerated web of nerves pleading for an early pardon.

They had been up late last night, she and Max. That greasy pit had indulged them until the doors were actually locked. They had sat at the rear booth while chairs were stacked on tables and the stench of ammonia sanitized the floor, their stomachs churning and cackling in deep-fry regret. The lights had dimmed to a conservative working level, while the volume from the kitchen rose in aggressive English and timid Spanish and banging cast iron. She hadn't even brought up the idea of getting out of the business—not especially after all the attention she had received earlier in that opera set restaurant. But in the midst of the everyday world, where the grilled cheese ruled the plate, and the purple darkness diminished the front window, she could see an end. The point where the young Sarah would turn to a fabled memory, freeing this Sarah from all responsibility of keeping the candle burning.

They had come a long way from passing their nights in opium dens, where they had tried to hang on long enough for the morning light to splinter, when they would crawl deathly toward their beds with the superiority of battered warriors claiming victory through their wounds. She was old now. Remarkable energy, intrepid spirit, and two layers of pancake could not disguise the fact that she had become an old woman. Her age was perhaps made diminutive by the youthful characters that she portrayed, and her brashness and reckless bullying that had introduced (and maintained) her reputation around the world. But in truth the edginess her life skated upon, the cold steel razor that at once chilled her veins and threatened to sever them, was now dulled and rusted and left out of view. Before, she had burned opium for enlightenment, seeing the present in a way that let it unroll and display itself as an entirely new vision, a new possibility that challenged itself through the ironies. But now when she smoked she was just a pathetic sixty-one-year-old hag, doped-up baggage that only weighted down the earth and slowed its turning. No wonder Max was concerned. She had turned from the rebellious boozer into the alleyway drunk, all because of a matter of thirty years that were nothing more than just the sum cumulative total of days passing.

She hadn't said so much to Max, but she had intimated that she was feeling wearied by this latest boycott, leaving it vague and open to interpretation. (Shouldn't it be obvious? Those kinds of melees are only really meant for the battle-excited young. Imagine, being exiled to the carnival!) Max immediately jumped on the opium issue, apparently sensing her openness as an invitation to express his concern, rather than any professionally motivated irritation. "The fact of the matter," he said, "is that the hop is terrible for you. Never mind your career, but just for your health and sanity. It's just bad."

Again, she wanted to tell him to stop saying *hop*. It sounded so juvenile and falsely vogue, and that the word came as stiffly off his mouth as a crippled old man holding on lustily to his buxom nursemaid. But then she realized that for most of her life her entire vocabulary had been a series of slang and exclusive nomenclature for the privileged insiders, only changing when the terms seeped across the borders and polluted the mainstream. Then there was some indefinable point—maybe a milestone— when the old words died away and the new ones seemed shallow or contrived, leaving the general formalities of the language to best express the details. "You are right," she said, restraining herself from correcting him. "Bad."

"It's just that it is so dulling."

She reached over and placed her hand on his forearm. Her sculpted fingers and thumb now bent slightly at the joints with the skin loosened, lines made deeper by the shadows from the dimmed lights. "I am telling you that I understand. It is not addiction, though. Just a way to cope." And as she said those words she felt an anger seethe through her body. The real Sarah Bernhardt, the younger version who hadn't been hideously taken over by this battered old-leathered shell, never needed to cope. If some freakish American church group had come after her, well then *je m'en fou!* That kind of thing would only serve to inspire the real Sarah. She would tease them, mug at them, and flaunt her virtues, then go out on the town to celebrate, spilling her points of view on the correlation of religious fanaticism and sold-out houses into the drinks and notes of every reporter who would listen. The best way to weather a shock had been to shock back (in her case in a way that reached the whole world). But this Sarah was rattled. Driven to panic and strange memories, where only the narcotics and booze could calm her. Bottom line: She couldn't take the pressure anymore. She didn't want to turn into an actress like Cissy Loftus, the kind of star whose perfection was her métier, but nobody could stand her, because when she wasn't arrogantly demanding perfection she was privately falling apart.

Max must have sensed the seriousness, because he quickly relaxed his managerial posture and leaned over more Molly-like, his rigid Saxon features softening, taking on a gentle femininity. He caressed her cheek. His hands, although still masculine, stroked with a comforting mercy that was neither patronizing nor sympathetic, rather one that bespoke honesty in its purest form, as though stoking her with true compassion. "You know that I love you" was all he said. And she understood the depth of those words so much that the literal was stripped of every nuance, the letters and phonetics falling away until they were no longer symbols of expression, but the pure, raw expression itself.

"I am old," she said.

Max slid his hand down her cheek and took hold of her hand, pressing it into the tabletop. "I don't even know what that means."

"You don't know old, Molly?"

He nodded. Almost convincingly.

"Just look in the mirror if you don't know old. And if you still don't get it, then look at me. Old is what it is, Molly . . . Old. I'm not going to be dancing side by side with Mata Hari, unless it's billed as a freak show."

"Sarah, you are not . . ."

"I'm not the Sarah Bernhardt that you want me to be." And with that he squeezed her hand, and she pursed her lips so tightly that they hurt, sealing off any other words that might slip out and reveal the brewing of rational and irrational fears that busked throughout her mind. Once exposed they might mutate and take on a life larger than she and Max could possibly imagine.

To the restaurant workers, they must have looked like an aging couple misplaced after the ball, conversations and discourse long ago exchanged, where the sharing of meals and long-gone expressions are ratified by a gentle touch that symbolizes intimacy. Sarah and her confidant Max sat silently in that deserted diner, his hand left gently on her forearm, their stares vacant and lone, while the floors around them were being mopped and the tables sprayed and sponged. And six thousand miles away among the sooty gray Parisian buildings lay a world that would still fawn over every word that their native daughter had to say. They would still line up at the window, crowding one another and pushing and pulling with a near hysterical determination to catch a glimpse of her. But here she sat with Max. An empty café in a deserted downtown Los Angeles. No less ordinary than any other couple who may have inadvertently found their way in. They could not have asked for a better moment of peace. And Sarah could only hold one thought. One single thought that swirled her mind like a playful pan that turned malicious and started banging the word against the cavity of her skull. One devious thought in two parts.

Old. And soon to be forgotten.

Even by the time they had flagged a taxi, she couldn't shake the thought. The suddenness of the restaurant's ambience had gone with the closing of the door and clacking of the lock. A warm gentle wind brushed up against her face and seductively wrapped her ankles. The dirty downtown smell oddly refreshing and inspiring. Still nothing could knock away the desperate vision of mortality that overcame her (compounded by having to sleep in circus town). She was glad Max was with her, because if ever there was a moment when she might have hooked herself up to a stash of opium and let it run until it whitewashed her existence, this was it.

The cab passed under a last streetlamp, which left Broadway looking unlucky and shadowed. The outlines of the giant palm leaves rose as ancient totem smiles. Sarah thought about closing her eyes, but it seemed like more work than just keeping them open. She watched until the cab quickly turned the corner on Second. The concrete cross from the Cathedral of our Lady of Angels stared down upon her, grainy gray, the edges chipped and rounded, and a footprint over the entrance. The name of the cathedral arced above, the once deep engraving now shallow and weathered. Sarah imagined Mother Superior reciting the creed to help herself find a calming peace, then marching right up to the bishop of this California parish to tell him how wildly mistaken he was, that her young novice was a girl of virtue and honesty, and despite a sometimes independent nature the young Mademoiselle Sarah was indeed a true conscript of the Father. (Although she too might have been tempted to give up on Sarah, finally conceding that the Jew in her could destroy all the potential goodness, unable to see that the same spark, the same gentleness and open heart that Sarah—or was it Henriette-Rosine?—had possessed at nine was still beating inside her chest.) Maybe the way that Sarah had gone about navigating the world was far more different than the sister could ever have imagined, but in the end they had both tried to achieve the same goals: to give up one's self for the love and salvation of others.

She reached down and took Max's hand. She looked back one more time at the church. It disappeared in shadows and night, as though it had never existed at all. "Please hold me until we get back to the hotel," she said.

"Sarah," he whispered, "we forgot to talk about Marguerite." She put her index finger to her lips. "Please just hold me."

She had gone to sleep rather easily in her room at the King George, the loathing and pity fully exhausting her. It was the morning that thwarted her. The nagging thoughts and blistered questions had sounded an alarm in her head. She tried to lull herself back to sleep with one of the many lullabies that her mother had once sung to her. Then she tried to relive her performances at the Odéon, where she had worked with the director, Félix Duquesnel. She had bombed her first time out (if the chill of the audience hadn't confirmed that then certainly

Duquesnel's harsh words did), but she persevered until that time in her career was probably her happiest. The rehearsals were often the most joyous—the camaraderie and promise that the cast shared made each day so full of life. They would sneak off between acts, having impromptu football games at Luxembourg, choosing teams based on roles, and trying to stay in character throughout the match. For the first time in her life feeling sweat running across her forehead, actually tasting laughter, and always leaving the grass stains on her knees to remind her of the sweet perfume of happiness. They would run the streets back, full of laughter and conceit, unknown to the world, but certain that their anonymity would be temporary. Mariette in *François le Champi* had been her real breakthrough. Nobody at the Odéon was afraid to tell her how good she had been, in fact they had rooted for her, stood in the wings, cheering her along with the crowd. And the crew encouraged her in *Le Marquis de Villemer* when Duquesnel had cast her as a baroness nearly twice her age. The rest of the ensemble called her Madame during the football games, and begged her royal pardon at all times. And she played it to the hilt. Even convincing herself that she was a middle-aged baroness on the verge of dementia, losing herself to her character, unable to see Duquesnel's smiles and encouragement when her character stormed off the stage, needing to open the stage door and let the cool breezes slap the Sarah back into her. If she had known how her life would turn out, she may never have left those days when the purity of the form was all that mattered. But, despite the camaraderie and seriousness, there was an implied drive for success. *The cream always rises to the top* is constantly whispered in your ear. That the real reason to hone your craft is in order to be a star. Nobody at the Odéon quite knew what a star was or meant, yet that was still the aim. Despite all her successes, Sarah never felt that she had been as pure an actor as when she was with the Odéon.

Sometimes those memories comforted her and put her right back to sleep.

Sometimes they only served to backlight the life she had ended up with, revealing all the contradictions and terrors that faced her each day.

Sarah couldn't fall back to sleep that morning. She closed her eyes again, picturing the newspaper headlines from two days ago. She imagined the planning and rallying going on in that church under the same moonlight. Worst of all, she kept seeing that young promising actress named Sarah Bernhardt at the Odéon being crushed under the mountainous rubble of what she had dreamed of being.

Ten past five. She kicked the covers off and walked into the bathroom. Bent her tired frame over to run the bath.

VINCE BAKER SLEPT FITFULLY. The night shot up at him in flits, reminding him that he was no longer dreaming. Each time he awoke the room was deep in a purple hue. And nothing felt familiar.

That's a lousy hangover for you. The kind that makes you think you're going to kick the booze forever.

The room smelled of locked-away boxes. His compass uncertain of which direction he actually faced, having to remind himself that he was even in Los Angeles and not Phoenix or someplace in between. But as the purple began to recede, some of the familiar forms started to take shape. The outline of the pile of unpacked boxes neatly stacked, the top one edged on a slight tilt. The almost unrecognizable rectangle of his couch, where the loose threads stuck out like hair from an old man's ear and beamed with unusual clarity. And the odd, almost phantasmal cone that he initially took for a mysterious apparition turned out to be nothing other than a pile of clothes overdue for drop-off at the Wash-Rite Laundry around the block. He sat straight up and looked to his side, where the familiar form of a female body lay under a solitary white sheet. Propped on her side, an even line from the peak of her shoulder to the curve of her hip, with the sheet sinking in four distinct wrinkle-waves. Her legs pulled back at a slight angle from her side, flowing straight down until the last bit of form was the slight crest of her foot, toeless under the sheet, cutting like a dancer's form. He looked at her and said the name Fay, drilling it into his head, as though reinforcing their artifice of familiarity.

By 5:00 A.M. he figured he repeated that same routine at least four times over the course of the night. No wonder his dreams were not evidence enough to convince him that he had actually had some sleep.

Baker gingerly lifted the covers to slide himself out. He parted the checked yellow curtains, the stained insides faded by sunlight, the dust rising, swirling, and twinkling in a strange mixture of fairy dust and filth.

He couldn't imagine the day extending any further than this moment. Maybe that's what suicides think before they actually turn out the lights. Perhaps their demise was not always due to a deep dark desperation that masked any inkling of hope, but instead a rational realization that they have hopped into the last possible square and it is literally impossible to imagine stepping anywhere beyond where they stand. He'd covered one suicide. A woman made memorable only by the fact that they shared the same last name was found slumped at the side of her bed in a nightly prayer posture, only her face had been crushed into a white duvet, stained red like a tissue from a bloodied nose. A small black gun rested nonchalantly at her side, as if it were supposed to be there, and when the detective gripped her hair and pulled her head up, there was a clean black hole through her right temple. A simple cease-fire message to the brain. Everybody knew that the female Baker had been pissed at G. G. Johnson and had intended to say something publicly. The problem was nobody knew what, and whatever it was had leaked out that little passage in her skull and spread thin across a bed that everybody knew Johnson had not-so-secretly shared. The LAPD reluctantly ruled it a suicide. Baker's story was boiled down to something resembling an obit that only ended up running in the Saturday bulldog edition. Both of the Bakers' story.

Today he just couldn't imagine going into the newsroom. The same musty smell, ragged smiles, and temporary pressures. It was a job that was practically impossible if you didn't submit to the illusion of it. Because once you faced that mirror, and for just one moment caught a glimpse of yourself, the ridiculousness of your righteousness and determination became laughable. Another living, breathing cliché. It was the deadlines with the intense pressure that kept the treadmill going. The sense that the moments were ticking away faster than you could keep up with them, daring you to fall behind and become completely lost and obsolete. Your snout had to sniff the ground at all times, tracking every scent, digging up every bone just in case one of them turned out to be something other than a butcher's scrap.

Baker's chest sank.

He couldn't imagine it. Not today.

He regretted not talking to Bernhardt last night. He could have accomplished two things: killed the story, and found out what the goddamn fascination was.

He crawled back into bed and curled up beside Fay. Holding on into the morning. Or at least until the next time he woke, almost screaming.

FOLLOWING A BATH that seemed merely functional, Sarah walked out of the lobby, past the sleepy-eyed desk clerk who between yawns probably only noticed the shadows, into a crisp morning whose breeze seemingly lifted right off the whitecaps. A pause held the pier.

She was alone.

Quietly and momentarily.

Her crew was due to arrive in the late morning, and Max would make sure the set was constructed to a workable phase in order that run-throughs could begin as soon as tonight. He was such a priss about things like this. They needed rehearsals, not run-throughs. They had done this play a hundred times already, and she had already meticulously blocked every movement and nuance down to the number of breaths per beat long before they had opened the tour. Everybody knew where they were supposed to be. But on a dramatic level the play was not quite working. After she talked it out with Max, the cast would need to work the changes through, scene by scene.

Marguerite Gautier was flat and the play was lifeless.

Yet the audiences didn't seem to care. They cheered because it was her. She could stand there speechless for three hours straight and they would still give her a minimum of ten curtain calls. Her presence had overshadowed her art. Why bother? She should just put it on celluloid for the Americans and forget about it. But until then the Sarah Bernhardt Company needed an organized and back-to-basics rehearsal. But Max would insist on a quick run-through instead. Just enough to make sure the set was comfortable for all. He would tell Sarah not to confuse the actors with her search for interpretations, that it was her approach that mattered, and that the actors would undoubtedly play their parts the same, only making the occasional emotional adjustment when necessary. But to concern them in a theoretical and philosophical discussion on the motives of Marguerite would only serve to confuse them and throw everything off-kilter. There were obligations to be met, and time did not allow for full-blown rehearsals. Max's rule was that everybody needed to be present at the run-through, even her dresser, Sophie, as though some siren wail of a costume emergency might sound, causing a needle and scissors resuscitation (along with the hairdresser, Ibé—which for him was no chore, as he literally spent every other night sleeping backstage on top of the wigs to protect them from lord knows what). But she knew Max was doing more than watching the crew, he was watching her, as well. Keeping sure that she didn't slip away. That's probably why he wanted her private railcar parked right down there on the pier. Always best to expose the hiding places.

This was her final bout of freedom. Bring on the crew by noon, and the wide-eyed cast by four. The first run-through starts at 5:00 P.M. sharp. It will go until 7:30 P.M., where they will break for dinner, customarily banquet style on the first night, where she is inevitably seated at the center table surrounded by Max and Sophie and the area promoter—in this case Abbot Kinney. A sense of unity is created at the dinners, where a group of stratified travelers are transformed into a single-mindedly focused acting troupe. Then Max stands up after the main course and welcomes everybody and introduces the promoter, who gushes with starstruck jealousy about the chills that shiver down his spine at just being in the room with such talent and brilliance, promising that packed houses and everything else you will need to ensure a first-class show is at your command. She can practically mouth the speeches along with their orators. (At least they are a little further and few between this time. On her first American tour she sometimes played four cities in five days. Four dinners. Four promoters giving four speeches.) Then the dinner breaks up around 9:30 P.M. and the actors all go off to discuss their concerns, and the production crew meets to resolve its problems with the latest theater. By the next morning, everything is in full swing again, as if they had been doing this every minute of their endless lives. She had traversed the United States several times now, pulled by a three-car train loaded with more than thirty of the best actors and crew that Europe had to offer, and she was certainly not lacking in confidence that the quality was pristine and perfect—without the promoter's benediction and blessing. The problem was these modern financiers who had figured out how to turn art into a slipshod celebrity commodity barely held together by the manipulation of the press, advertising, and rumor. They never once thought about quality or talent or innovation. There was no suggestion of nuance and subtlety—in fact, more the opposite: where only the biggest loudest bang could stretch the pockets deeper. The promoters had managed to put a fear of God into Max that created the illusion that profit margin was equivalent to quality. Almost always leaving poor Molly to run around after the show, balancing reviews against the ledgers to determine the night's success. It usually took the train ride with the crew to slap the perspective back into him.

For this she gives up a rehearsal.

Sarah sat down on a bench that faced Kinney's Chautauqua Theater, the stage door far off to the right, almost hanging over the Pacific. By the closing curtain that entrance surely would be mobbed with people climbing over one another to get a look at her and have her scribble her name in a diary or any other keepsake they could muster. They would enunciate their words in loud English to translate fully their adoration, and then inevitably part with some canned wisdom like *don't let them get you down* or *don't worry you'll always be great.* Those moments of adulation after the performance tended to be her loneliest. There she stood in grace and charm, her smile radiating something larger than life, reaching her hands over to delicately touch fingertips and palms. Her lips repeatedly mouthed *merci* with no sound vibrating her throat, driven by the insatiable need not to stop. She rarely enjoyed it though because she was always so hyperaware that it would eventually end with Molly breaking it up. She could stay out there all night in a mechanical rhythm if he didn't always announce very loudly, "Thank you very much, but Madame Bernhardt needs her rest," keenly aware of the perception of maintaining a demand. Then she would walk away, having blown kisses, mouthing more silent *mercis*, and delivering a final wave. Then the loneliness and ennui would set in predictably, burrowing deep into her chest. Raising smiles seemed impossible when she finally joined the cast in a throwaway suite or private dining room for the after-performance party. Drugs. Booze. Sex. The usual remedies to see an actor through until morning. She really had become too old for that nonsense. Just lead her to the railcar and let her be.

A few people started to appear in the distance. Probably heading for work. Not far from Sarah, a wide woman passed. She walked low to the ground in short, terse steps, unaware that there was another person around her. And by the Ferris wheel a stoop-shouldered man trailed by his long narrow shadow dragged slowly and disinterestedly. Sarah heard the sounds of morning. The cackles of electricity opening the stores and offices. The seagulls barking and howling as they glided in first flight over the pier. And she looked back at the hotel, the bright orange sun hitting the windows in the middle—maybe her window even—and splashing the entire front in a blaze that transformed it into a strange beacon that called Sarah Bernhardt to duty.

She didn't want to go back.

She didn't want to wait for Max's predictable tap on the door at 8:30 A.M. to escort her to the breakfast room.

She didn't want to hear about Catholics and their boycotts.

She didn't want to have to smile and greet Abbot Kinney and feign gratitude.

She didn't want to go over and over all the necessary preparations with Max and the crew.

She didn't want to struggle to understand Marguerite Gautier.

She wanted to walk with some purpose. Have her shadow drag reluctantly behind. Uncertain of what the day would bring, but definite that it wouldn't leave her chest hollow.

These few days on her own had made her appreciative of having no commitment to time. And she wished that she were going to set herself at the edge of the pier with a fishing rod in hand, ready to catch her breakfast. But no doubt that would never happen here again. Maybe if Kinney had just left her alone that morning everything would have been as peaceful and personal as she had intended. But he had wanted to make a show of it, so she had given him a show.

Instead she walked back. In honor of duty. Head hung low. Her body slumped nearly unrecognizable. She moved straight toward the orange light. Guided into the beacon. Driven by the knowledge that once she walked through those doors she would be Sarah Bernhardt again. And she would rise to the occasion. Square her shoulders, adjust her stature, and open herself up wide to take all the shit that could possibly be hurled—along with all the adulation that would keep her whole.

Max was standing in the lobby as she walked through the doors. His expression crossed between irritation and relief. "Do you know what time it is?" he asked, parentally.

She smiled and clutched his shoulders, pulling herself up to give him a peck on the cheek. "Was my Molly getting a little hungry? Such a temper when you're hungry." (Frightening how she can become "Sarah" so quickly and on demand.)

"The train arrives in less than an hour and a half."

"And . . . ? I think this Abbot Kinney has you dreaming about him and his ledgers."

The lobby was beginning to fill, mostly with workers, a few tourists, and the privileged trend-setting indigents who called this glamour hotel their home. The foyer moved at a vacation pace, lazy and deliberate, with slow smiles of recognition between familiar faces and casual greetings with loosely knit plans. Quite in contrast to Max Klein. He and Sarah stood in the center of the room in an inert pause—the frantic eye to an otherwise calm storm, both daring each other to say another word. She sensed a shift in the room's mood, the familiar sudden breathlessness when all eyes have convergently focused on her. And instinctively, with grace and demur, she inflated her presence to three times her petite size. The fluidity of her gestures and expressions turned artful as she leaned in closer to Max, aware of the exact volume of her movements as though it were a mathematical equation (*size of room × proximity of people ÷ distance of audience = projected volume*) and kicked her back leg up in a natural gesture that carried the understated exaggeration of comedy—just enough to let the audience find her both sophisticated and charming. She spoke in a stage whisper an inch before his ear, "I am positively famished. Should we retire to the dining room"—she pulled in closer to complete the line for only him to hear—"before these gawkers eat me alive?" And Max, being Max, announced in what would have been seen as an overdone and overcompensating voice to anybody other than a starstruck room, "But of course, Madame. To the dining room." And the crowd parted with the nonchalance of eavesdroppers, knowingly letting her pass, leading the way a step behind Max Klein, who was undoubtedly waiting for her to stop at any moment and say she only had a few minutes for autographs and questions. For the next half hour until he made the customary announcement.

"THE EGGS ARE COLD," she said. "They have only been on my plate for what, a minute or two? They are cold. Are yours cold too, Molly?"

Max finished chewing what had been his first bite. Masticating with increased effort until he could force the food down his throat. "Mine are fine," he finally was able to answer. The same scrambled eggs, shining lemon yellow, spread generously along the plate next to three strips of thick, sizzling bacon with the white fatty part puffed at the ends, and two thick slices of a dense brown bread (she had called it an Irish breakfast at first sight). "They are fine."

"But you always say that."

"Because it's true."

"Because you are afraid."

"Afraid?"

"Of offending."

"Whom? Surely not you."

"Hardly." She smiled. "But the waiters."

"What are you saying?"

"That you would rather eat cold eggs than complain. You don't want to upset the waiters."

"Sarah, that is not true at all. I happen to think that they are at an ideal temperature for consumption."

"The lengths you'll go to convince yourself."

"When the food comes out burning hot you can't eat it anyway. You have to let it cool down, right? Well, this is the ideal eating temperature. There are no issues of embarrassment or apprehension. In fact, there are no issues at all."

"Well, it causes you to have to eat faster."

Max had just taken another bite and was chewing with a slower, more deliberate determination.

"There is only a finite amount of time when the temperature is ideal. Do you follow?"

Max nodded without commitment.

"When it comes out too hot then you can savor it. A little breath to cool it down. Talk. Enjoy. Then another bite. Still hot. Again a little less breath to cool it down. But the way you like it, one has to devour it almost immediately or else it becomes impossible to enjoy. It's a matter of something being able to stay around for a long time to be enjoyed, and something else being garbled and mangled because its moment of satisfaction is so visibly temporary."

He swallowed. "I get it," he said. "Do you want me to order you another dish? Send it back to the kitchen?"

"It's just that this is ludicrous. Does their Chef Louis find this acceptable?"

"I will try to get the waiter's attention."

"It shouldn't be hard. He has been staring at us unremittingly since we sat down."

"He is in awe of you."

"Or he knows that the eggs are cold."

Max turned around to survey the room. "I will try to get his attention."

"And when you do, explain to him what I have told you. Or tell him that it's just like sex. You want the passion to keep burning so you can continue to take little bites and tastes along the night. Or is that how it works with you boys, Molly? Perhaps you men-to-men are the epitome of male aggression, baring your teeth in full savagery, grunting for pleasure and mounting each other in pure ready-to-eat convection. Gnaw and destroy in a matter of moments. Is that how it is? In a way it all makes perfect sense. At least sexually, almost all men believe that women think just like men. That the pleasures are uniformly shared and that everybody wants the same thing. So perhaps it does follow that men would do better with men.

They are actually choosing the right partner to fulfill their suppositions and expectations. In a way that is beauty in an aesthetic of logic. Does that sound right to you? Is that how it is?"

Max chose to ignore her. "I see him coming out of the kitchen now. I think . . ." He waved his hand politely.

"Of course," she continued, "all the queer men I have been with, and I had a few—some before they were willing to admit it, others who wanted to believe I was a man, and others who would do anything at any time—they seemed to like their food served hot. They wanted to dine. What is the answer, Molly? What *is* the truth?"

"Here he comes." Max explained the issue to the waiter, whose fat, round face burst red in a combination of discomfiture and rage at the notion of his guest's disappointment. He was truly and terribly sorry and hoped that this would not disrupt her morning. It would only be a few minutes, but was there anything else that he could bring in the meantime? And he started to back away, unable to distract his attention from Sarah's face, the chapter-and-verse definition of starstruck. "Oh," he paused, "would the gentleman also like a fresh plate? Is it not warm enough either?"

"Well, Molly?" Sarah asked. "We are all waiting to know the answer."

Max shook his head and rolled his eyes. "Please," he said. "Please."

"I wouldn't have figured it, Molly. I'd have thought you as stubborn as me."

"That's why I'm in charge, Madame. The very reason why."

The waiter stood by the table. His eyes trained on Sarah. "I believe that was a yes, dear," she said to him.

"My apologies." He looked flustered. "It's just that . . . One moment, please." He began to back away from the table.

"Pardon me." Sarah spoke again. "Are you going to remove the plates?"

"Oh dear, indeed," he said, reaching over to scoop up her plate, then placing Max's on top, smothering hers, bacon tips peeking out the side. "Your presence just startles me."

"I will trade you a signature for a hot plate of food. Is that fair? My trusted Max will find a cabinet photo for you that I can deface with my scribble."

He nodded twice and backed away, looking at her the whole way.

"See, Molly, that was not so hard. Everybody understands that it is better to have things served hot. Endurance and longevity. Almost inevitably more important than talent."

"And speaking of, we have to get the show in order."

"Oh here we go."

"Sarah, you will have had nearly a week between shows. Even you must admit that makes the potential for some sloppiness. But a brief run-through is all we need. It is not necessary to tax the actors so much."

"They need more than to just familiarize themselves with the set."

"The set is a whole other matter."

"What we need to figure out is Marguerite's relationship to her consumption. Does it control her? Is it the impetus to give her more conviction? Does it make her love Duval stronger, or more distant? When I was younger I saw that disease as part of her strength. That the contradiction of it empowered Marguerite to take on the world with more passion. Again, I am not certain. I am not even certain of the motive of the disease. But to expect that Armand Duval reacts to Marguerite the same no matter how she envisions herself is ludicrous. It alters the emotional staging of the entire play. It is not just about blocking, and making sure that all the props are in place, in order to save cuddle time with the promoters."

Sarah and Max turned around, expecting to see the waiter but instead saw Abbot Kinney. He smelled of the cleanliness of fine soaps and imported cologne, and his demeanor announced a diligence for perfection. He was both manners and forceful drive. He stood politely with his right hand speared through his trouser pocket, the other fixed at his side. "I have just heard about your breakfast. And I hope to adequately convey the embarrassment of the entire staff by offering this apology. But rest assured, your meals will be arriving shortly. And if they are not satisfactory, then we will crack every egg between here and Mexico until we are certain that you are fully content with your breakfast."

"Quite all right," Max said.

"Or I could just go catch some sea bass," Sarah added. She was the only one who laughed. Kinney looked away. Max stared hard at her.

Kinney gripped the back of a free chair. "Do you mind if I join you for a few minutes? As there are some matters facing the day." He pulled the chair before the formal invitation was issued, setting himself between Max and Sarah. "Your crew is due to arrive midmorning. Is that right?"

"Both the actors and the crew," Max corrected.

"And you'll begin working in the theater today?"

"That is our plan. A solid run-through."

"I am genuinely elated at the notion that my theater will soon be transformed into the Parisian stage. Genuinely. Now is there anything I can do? I intend to be there during the day to help, and make myself available."

Max glanced quickly to Sarah.

"Anything?" Kinney asked.

"The only thing that I am concerned about besides getting Madame's car down to the pier," Max said, trying to gain the upper hand, "is in making sure that we have a spotlight that is ready and working. I believe in the contract you said that you would furnish the necessary supplies for the lime light."

"And remind me of those again."

"We have the equipment, but we asked you to supply the calcium carbonate."

Kinney reached for a pad and pen from his breast pocket. "Now let me write this down. Calcium carbonate."

"Lime," Max said. "It's the name for lime."

"I do remember now. I have one of my staff on it, in fact. For some reason he has had some difficulty in locating it, but last I heard there was hope with a builder in Pasadena. Is it absolutely necessary?"

"It will not work without the mineral. And yes, it is absolutely necessary to staging the show. Madame Bernhardt"—he spoke as though she were not there—"is fully committed to the aesthetic of selective realism. The entire play is designed around the stylized set that suggests the essence of the era and location. She sees it as another character." Max continued to explain the importance of the concept, no doubt posturing to gain the respect and position of Abbot Kinney, and then he launched into the science of the calcium carbonate (*lime*, he kept clarifying, in order to reinforce his expertise) and the oxyhydrogen torch, and how the heat creates the incandescence, continuing on with all the nuances that only the most skilled craftsmen could truly master.

Sarah drifted in and out of the conversation, not wishing to involve herself in the power struggle that was playing out in front of her. She laughed to herself at the notion of someone who barely understood science explaining it to someone also equally ignorant, and how their mutual nescience seemed to oddly bond them. Max didn't talk like this when they had gone to visit Thomas Edison during that first tour of America. In fact, Max didn't speak a word, equally terrified at being seen as gay as at being identified as simple. They had been playing *La Dame aux Camélias* in New York, and that particular performance had extended nearly an hour. Seventeen curtain calls after the third act. Twenty-nine after the fifth. New York has always appreciated her. And somehow in the midst of all this, the promoter Jarrett had arranged for Sarah to meet Thomas Edison at his home in Menlo Park, New Jersey. Jarrett had clearly thought that there were some good photos and press to be had, and he basically hoodwinked both parties into the summit, convincing each megastar that the other wanted to have the honor of the meeting. Max had been opposed from the start (given they had to leave New York in the morning for Boston), but even then he was especially afraid of contradicting a promoter. So out they rode in the middle of the night, wearing tomorrow's traveling clothes (just in case), with the snow falling, and the carriage sliding almost sideways the entire trip, the tread barely catching the ice.

They finally reached his home at some unusual hour, and she remembered seeing it lit up on the hill, the incandescent lights glowing, showing off the white of the multistory home and making the dark shutters look even darker. The carriage pulled through the picket fence with the opening curiously at the house's side. When they got out, Edison and his wife, Mary, were both waiting on the porch, alongside a newspaper reporter and some other local dignitaries. Mary had been fairly gracious, almost speechless when faced with the stage star, but Edison, in contrast, had appeared to be cold and stiff. He politely took Sarah's hand and respectfully shook Max's, but his diffidence was loud and clear. It's not like Sarah had really wanted to be there either. She had just come off one of the shows of her life and would have rather celebrated the success in a Manhattan nightclub than on a carriage bound for New Jersey. But there she was. And there he was. Younger and not quite as thoughtful-looking as she might have imagined.

It was clear from his expressions and lack of conversation that Edison had been expecting a host of idiotic questions about his inventions followed by a few smiles and quotes for tomorrow's papers. She knew it by his eyes. She understood the feeling of being trapped in a room with people who know what you do but have so little understanding, and then think a few basic questions and a twenty-minute tête-à-tête will make it all clear. It displayed little regard for the intellect and training and practice and study that were all labored over for years and years; instead it was concocted into a final product that appeared so basic in its shamelessness.

Question: *How do you do it?*

Answer: *Well, how do you breathe?*

Edison had been so prepared for the bombardment that he didn't consider he was facing someone who experienced the same issues.

At one point in the evening, after many of the guests had

gone, Sarah had been wandering the house and ended up in her host's study, tracing titles on the bookshelf. She felt a presence behind her and turned to see the inventor. "I was just admiring your collection of Shakespeare," she had said. "I am impressed and intrigued by the fact that you have five different volumes of Hamlet."

"When I finish reading it, I go out and buy another," he explained. "That way I never feel like I am rereading it. It is always a fresh book. Each time I am so moved by his indecision, by the crossroads of emotion and reason."

"I have played Hamlet countless times, and I understand exactly what you feel."

"I envy you. I would do anything to have the opportunity just to feel what it is like to suffer Hamlet's indecision."

"Perhaps you could invent it."

With that Edison laughed. His shoulders had relaxed, and for one moment he opened his eyes wide enough to appreciate that he was in the presence of someone who understood. "Would you like to see my lab?" he asked. And then he took her hand and guided her out a side door, away from the social farces, out into the snow and down the road to his compound of invention. They trudged through the snow, past the office library and into the lab, just in front of the machine shop that bordered the railroad tracks that he said ran toward Mine Gully. He twisted a switch, and light spilled through the room from the incandescent lamps attached to the inverted T-shaped gas fixtures from the ceiling. It was almost a Provence glow, made soft by the streaking sheen along the slatted wood ceiling and matching floors. Then she saw rows of tables with dining room legs, topped by test tubes, wires, stray bits of glass, and rows of tools that all looked like variations of tweezers. In the back of the room sat a pipe organ, whose glowing brass pipes ascended on the right until the final tube nearly touched the ceiling. The room smelled sweetly of grease and oil, and the intangible fragrance of passion and intellect.

"I am honored," she said.

"Over here." He motioned her to the front table. His eyes both charming and mad. "Sit here."

Before her sat a beautiful base of polished wood, and balanced across the top was a brass-looking cylinder with two mismatched ends, one jutting out like the wide barrel of a pistol, and the other squat and mechanical. A masterwork of sculpture. "This is your phonograph?" she asked with awe in her voice.

He merely smiled, then touched his bent fingers to the apparatus and worked the small machinery. He looked up at the ceiling while his recorded voice, distant and mangled, was heard singing "Mary Had a Little Lamb" through the open-mouth cone.

Sarah let out a laugh. A glorious freeing laugh from all the pressures and expectations and loneliness that had accompanied her magnifying glass tour. Tears formed in her eyes as she felt the beauty and imagination of possibility that was singing to her in a shaky off-key voice. It was all she could do not to hug him. "Thank you," she said, once the song had ended. And never before in her life had the words innately carried the gratitude that their true meaning intended.

"Now may I ask a favor of you?" His voice had the quivery quality of the recording. He looked down at his brown shoes that tapped the floor. "Would you recite something from *Hamlet* for me?"

"It would be my honor." She moved between the row of

tables and stopped before the organ. She looked to her audience of one, a lone figure of appreciation with the mind of a thousand, and recited Hamlet's soliloquy from the third act *To be, or not to be* and when she finished *Be all my sins remember'd* she stayed in character and then rerecited the speech in French, *Etre ou ne pas être*. When she finished she saw Edison's eyes filled by tears—almost miraculously the same ones that had been in hers. He looked at her with a sadly joyous smile and nodded his head, as though it were a standing ovation.

She walked off her imaginary stage and they met in the middle of the room, joined by a passion that was not sexual, but rather of the beauty of dedication and belief. And he took both her hands and held them in honor, and she swore she felt the electricity that he had sent into those lightbulbs travel along every nerve ending in her body.

"I suppose that we should go back," she said. "It is getting late, I'm sure."

"My wife will keep them entertained. Unless you are getting tired. Two performances in one night. We should do three— and record the third. How about a monologue that combines English and French. Is that possible?"

"It is a long trip back to New York, right?"

"You would be lucky to be back at your hotel by midnight in this weather. You might as well stay and enjoy the evening. You are out here already." He walked up to the organ and opened the seat. He removed a book of sheet music and then produced a small brown bag. The bench slammed shut as he walked back to the table where Sarah was waiting. He crinkled the top of the bag into a funnel and poured a fine white powder along the surface. "Have some so you can enjoy the rest of the night." And together they both inhaled the cocaine, tasting the bittersweet powder on the backs of their tongues, before it clogged their throats and fully awakened them.

The hit freed Sarah like a claustrophobic from a closet. She felt her body lift from a solid form. Breath flowed through her mouth and straight through her pores, as though there were no need for lungs, but instead for a cleansing. And with that her chest turned hollow and light, her breasts inverting and disappearing until her essence of femininity had graciously stepped aside, liberated by a sexless purity. She realized how tight her body had been. Her neck muscles gripped in one last squeeze before fully releasing themselves. Her eyes felt softer, and the inside of her head buzzed in liberation, as though some other extra being had taken up residence there. And when she looked up at the ceiling, she swore that she saw the world-famous Divine Sarah Bernhardt floating freely, throwing back the occasional reassuring smile, letting her know that all was okay.

"What is it like," Edison asked, "to be a woman playing Hamlet?"

"The theater, like much of the world, is obsessed with difference. No matter what the essence of the art is, the issue is always turned back to novice aesthetics. Can a woman play a man? Can an old woman play a young girl? Critics have the audacity to compare my Hamlet to Booth's—bit by bit, male versus female—and he hasn't played it for fifteen years. They would never have done that with another man. Art is always being judged without ever considering the art."

"Even machinery must be critically interpreted, it appears. And most people seem unwilling to accept the unexpected."

"Please." She dropped her head back and laughed. "They are still talking about it. I have never seen anything like it. Face the truth. Everybody, whether they care to admit it or not, is sick and bored with the usual Booth Hamlet, played by both Edwin and his father before him. Strong, yet melancholy. Shy, but romantic. Gravely serious with every reaction. Hamlet was a boy, barely a man. And they played him as though he were weighted by the souls of a thousand lifetimes. I make him a boy. Impetuous. Curious. Give him some humor. I make him real."

"What do you do to bring out the childishness?"

"Little things. When Polonius wants to sit beside me, I kick my feet up on the chair to keep him away. I don't do the old school scooting away in gentle cowardice. This is now a deliberate boy. I run. I jump. I skip. I make even the most frightening moments for Hamlet filled with wonder."

"Your Hamlet is happy?"

"Of course not. He is sad. It is tragic. But still he is impulsive, and reacts like a boy would. He plays at revenge. He does not mastermind it. He is a sad, sad boy. But he plays with every situation like a toy to try to make himself feel life. It is nuance that speaks loudest."

The room carried a strange haze that discolored the black, only clearly visible in waving plumes across the electric lights.

Edison stared up at the ceiling. Smiling to himself, before drawing his expression into a stern but thoughtful expression. And though his skin was still taut from youth, his face looked old, as if the ghosts of wisdom and hardship had laid permanent rest. He was fragile and worn. Something that there is always beauty in. "This age of invention," he began, "is not so much different. We take inanimate objects, and through manipulation create meaning. Right? We place a needle into a wax cylinder, and the friction that is created we accept as music. Or the incandescence of filaments and electricity as sunlight. We have to choose to believe our interpretations. Otherwise, there is only a needle grinding into wax."

"This is what you think about in your workshop?"

Edison laughed.

She reached over and took his hand. There was nothing sensual or maternal in the touch. Two comrades falling through space, holding on boldly and passionately to make the landing more graceful. Edison squeezed her hand. And for a moment, that flesh and bones coupler of interlaced fingers was all that ground them to the earth. In a workshop in New Jersey. Where genius flowed so discreetly. Two wayward stars looking for a galaxy.

They did not leave the lab for another hour. Edison talked about how he always imagined the rhythm and structure of Shakespeare's poetry with each invention that he was working on, knowing that the same balance and science of intricacy could be applied to both, while Sarah laughed and slapped the table, exclaiming at the irony that she only saw the fineness of invention in her art (and also mentioned that recently she had become intrigued by sculpting in order to be able to touch and feel the art). And where candles would have dimmed to suggest the passing of the hours, the electric lights burned bright and timeless.

When they finally got back to the house at half past two, Max and Edison's wife were left sitting alone together, facing each other in sleepy silence, each with their own aggravations. Mary Edison's fiery jealousy could be witnessed by her refusal to make eye contact with her husband. Her resentfulness was not rooted in the fear of infidelity, but in the betrayal of her husband's isolated and private world, which she had ascribed to his genius. In fact, *jealous* may not have been the right word; instead maybe it was shock. The shock of discovering that her Thomas's insular world was penetrable—just not by her.

And poor Molly. He was twisted and contorted in his chair, arms folded against his chest, his legs crossed tightly and kicked under the seat, as though closing himself off from any intimate conversation that might accidentally come his way in the deep and silent night. His greeting was one of relief and of frightened disappointment. In fact, he had whispered in her ear in French something to the effect that he was worried that she was going to leave him here all night drowning in dilettante discourse. Mary Edison offered a cordial but not forthright invitation to stay in the guest room, but the waiting coach (which was on the clock that only got punched in New York) was the saving excuse. They parted quickly. Standing on the porch under a light snowfall that diamond sparkled in the lamplight, each offered cultured graciousness in their farewells. Sarah forgot to thank her host formally for such an inspiring and magical evening. As she stepped off the porch, Edison ran after her, slipping on the last step and gripping the banister for balance. Mary Edison looked away. Max Klein hustled into the carriage ("we will be lucky to get back to the Albemarle Hotel by four A.M.," he grumbled, "and then we're sure to be a wreck for Boston"). Edison grabbed onto Sarah's arm. He forgot to make the recording, he had said. She thought she would cry.

The next afternoon's dailies hardly reported on it.

No conflict. No drama.

No drama. No news.

The hotel waiter served Sarah's plate over her right shoulder, and then followed with Max's. Abbot Kinney broke the conversation to say, "Thank you, Anthony," before returning his attention to Max's authoritative yet lacking dissertation on the science of the lime light. Sarah leaned over to paddle the eggs' rising steam toward her. She took in the buttered perfume and let it awaken her stomach, allowing the steam to wash over her face. She barely heard Kinney when he asked, "Much more satisfactory now, Madame?"

She looked over at him without raising her head, and in her most rehearsed role of gentility and public manners, she told him that they were *parfait*.

"And by the way," Kinney added, "I have spoken with some of my press contacts and it appears that this immoral business from those loudmouth Catholics will not have any effect on the box office here. Ticket sales are brisk."

She blew delicately over her fork, watching the heat disappear. "That is good news." She took the first bite, feeling the comfort and satisfaction of eggs properly cooked.

"We were really not worried on that account," Max added. "I would say that nearly every tour that we have been on in the United States has seen some group that has cried out that Madame Bernhardt is immoral. In fact, we might even start to question ourselves if we didn't hear that. We certainly plan it into our publicity budget. Right, Madame?"

"The American free press. Can't take sides. Standing on the high wire of objectivity," she said.

"Well," Kinney stated, "I would suspect that we have benefited more than the bishop on this one."

"The bishop," she muttered. "The bishop . . . Do you know the expression 'stage business,' Monsieur Kinney?"

"I confess my lack of theater knowledge."

"An actor conveys her meaning in two ways: one, by the way she delivers her lines, and two, by the small unscripted things that she does with her body. The way she fiddles with her hands. Or how she picks things up and puts them down again. Or the way she blows smoke rings. The combination of little gestures tells the audience so much about the character—often by contradiction, or sometimes by reinforcement."

"Madame," Max tried to cut her off.

"I have been asking Max this very question." She turned to her manager: "You must be so tired of hearing it." Then she focused back on Kinney. "What do you think this bishop was doing when he spoke to the press? They are always the contradiction, those of the higher order. They speak the words so eloquently and piously from the script, often with a curse of virtuous indignation thrown in for emphasis. But the little things they do tell you the real truth about them. What do you imagine this Bishop Conaty was doing with his hands?"

"I wouldn't know," Kinney replied, clearly enjoying the revival of the younger Sarah.

"He probably kept a hand innocently rested on his robe. And each time he talked with more passion, I will bet that he tickled his crotch. Talking of decency while actively pursuing his own indecency, thereby fueling the passion for his hatred of me. People like me just reinforce his shame."

Max cut her off. "As I said, this is all in typical fashion. A little jousting match to try to draw attention. Only Madame is evidently much more skilled than any of her adversaries."

Max was really starting to sound idiotic right now. In his effort to keep from being upstaged by Kinney, he was starting to turn into Kinney, all brash and strutting, telling war stories to build his character. And while it was true that they had dealt with this shit throughout her career, it was also true that those kooks had never been able to claim success before. But now they had kept her from playing in Los Angeles. Successfully exiled her from maybe the second greatest theater town in the States. Booted her hapless ass out to circus town. And while Max was prattling on with his own version of reality he had also forgotten that his center stage diva was a lot older now. He still lived the illusion of the impudent Sarah. When they decried her as ghoulish, she had had Max arrange to have Nadar take publicity photos of her in a coffin. If they said she conveyed debauchery, well next time she would lower her neckline a little. But people had grown immune to the vitriol, they hardly noticed that her brazenness had started to retreat now that she was older. They didn't even talk about it anymore, and if they did it was in this same tone of bravado defiance that Max was adopting and that Kinney was loving. It is no wonder she found herself craving opium. Even at this early hour.

As they sat making plans for when the company arrived, Kinney and Max started looking like a couple to her, only she wasn't sure if Kinney was starting to look like a full-on queer, or if Max was butching himself into a full-blown Max. Either way she needed to remind herself to talk to him about that ass that he was making of himself. She listened for a few minutes to their detailed logistics, and then took another bite. She closed her eyes and let the ghost steam rise over to seal them shut. If she couldn't see it then it wasn't there.

FAY HAD LEFT WITH VINCE BAKER in the morning. Walked out the front door by his side and kissed him good-bye on *his* goddamned porch steps. Unbelievable. She actually had had the gall to get out of bed and play house. After she cleaned up some of the dishes to make some room on the kitchen counter, she had managed to take his lone egg and three pieces of bread and stretch them into a minimal breakfast for two. Covered in his white terry robe for privacy, Baker could barely eat. Fay was watching him. She had had that falling look in her eye. The dreamy one. The princess in the castle who had been kissed by prince charming, thereby releasing the broad and tramp in her out into the night. Some castle. And some princess. She had a sweet face and all, good size hips with a pair of legs to dream about, but let's face it, she and he had spent most of their night smashed on booze and hope, and for the better part of the evening they had hardly been two compassionate loving human beings bent on connection, but rather lonely hollow frames commanded by the crap they had ingested to hold each other in order to pass the night. Love and commitment were not exactly part of the arrangement.

Baker started to head into the office, but the truth was he didn't really care anymore about the fucking *Herald* and Los Angeles water-money politics or hearing about his phantom Sarah Bernhardt story. What he really cared about was getting a real amount of food and coffee into his system so he could feel partway normal and relieve the buzzing in his head.

Out on the sidewalk, the salty air made its way through the city streets and bent the tops of the palms so forcefully that it seemed they might break in their fragility. And while Baker usually would head downtown to C. C. Brown's and sit at the counter leaned over old-man style and inhaling the steam of the coffee, trying not to be blinded by the shining white tile floors, he couldn't go there because Fay had taken the morning shift, and if he walked back in she would surely think he was riding in with the stinking glass slipper nestled somewhere between his crotch and his heart. Damn if she had to be working last night. A little self-control can go a long way—especially when taking the long run into account. Now C. C. Brown's had to be placed on hiatus until the blood and pheromones cooled down. The typical strategy of avoidance would have to be employed until Fay's romance turned to anger, then to disappointment. Then he could show up again and feign being the object of her pity for men.

He paced the sidewalk. Trying to figure out where he could go for food, safe from women, and safe from politicos. Once his belly was full, then he would try to figure out how he was going to ram his fist right up Graham Scott's ass and get back onto the water wars. His story would not be blown by the screwups of the *Herald* newsroom and their idiocies at the Vienna Buffet over a year ago. The real issue at hand was the corporate barons standing to make a fortune over control of the valley's water supply. But then maybe that is what the Mahogany Row boys were afraid of. Don't want to bite off the hand that may feed you. Fear is a newspaperman's poison pill. And the entire goddamn newsroom was popping them like candy. They ought to have their own Hippocratic oath about keeping their constituents free from harm and injustice, and not hide their heads between their legs at the first sign of trouble or questioned advertisers' dollars. One would think there was some accountability to truth and justice in this business.

He'd straighten all this out.

If he ever got his strength back.

Abbot Kinney's Chautauqua Theater. The name and its namesake both filled suddenly with life. Kinney stood near the entrance to the floor proudly watching Sarah Bernhardt's company disperse throughout the auditorium. They were like a tactical unit. Specially trained and skilled in their purpose and mission. And though few at first sight had the grace and sophistication of their leader (upon arrival they looked like ragamuffin clowns, with their tousled hair and oversize, rumpled clothes featuring a combination of patterns and bright colors that brought Kinney back to his European days), once they assumed their posts, huddled in their conferences, and began orienting for the various tasks, they looked as proficient as any successful professionals.

He watched Madame Bernhardt skulking by the front of the house, her expression bored and defiant. Pacing sternly along the right side of the stage, then stopping to lean back and drift her stare vacantly to the rafters. Occasionally one of the clowny stagehands would approach her in obvious nervousness, standing patiently to ask her opinion. Bernhardt would listen with her chin held up properly, punctuating her attention with a slight but mannered nod. And she never once looked directly at the stagehand. Her eyes remained focused on the ceiling, except for when she drew them down to emphasize disapproval or surprise. This time, as with the others, she threw her hands up in the air and turned her head in a cliché of French disgust. The stagehand walked away when her arms finally lowered, and she began pacing again, fidgeting her fingers at her side. And though Kinney was suspect of her ability to manage her life at any higher degree than that of a blind, flatulent lapdog, he could not deny the power of her luminescence as it filled the room—even in such a moment of ordinariness.

Max Klein walked up to Kinney. "It is amazing, isn't it? How the hands of men can transform an empty room into a breathing village so easily."

Kinney nodded. "Is Madame Bernhardt upset?" he asked. Klein seemed barely capable of maintaining her. From where Kinney stood, it seemed like the diva walked right over her manager day and night. It's a wonder Max Klein never went the other way and ended up married, for how much he appeared to like to be stepped on by women.

"Why would you ask?"

"You are making sure she is content, right? I would just like everything to run smoothly from this point on. Although I don't think a little public outburst now and again regarding the bishop would be the worst thing to happen to us. But let's make sure that we plan for it. No more chances with the press."

"I will make sure to relay that to her . . . Is her car parked along the pier?"

"I saw it myself."

"It is good for occasions of momentary solace. Sometimes even the sun needs to hide behind the clouds for a while."

"Well, I look forward to seeing her shine."

"You will soon see Sarah's brilliance. There are just some technical difficulties to be determined. Differences of opinions, you know."

"Is it the hall?"

"It is more a matter of having an empty hall. It leaves more room for discussion."

"The auditorium is fine, I hope?" Kinney asked.

"The auditorium is fine."

"And Madame Bernhardt?"

"I have told you—she too is fine."

Kinney said he was glad to hear it. Since the episode on

the pier he had had a needles-and-pins stomach about this performance. He really did not have any secrets, nothing to hide about his business dealings and such, in fact he had made the point with all his accountants that every transaction and deal that had been made to bring Venice of America to life should be free and clear of malfeasance. He had worked hard to keep a clean reputation, limiting his newspaper contacts to benign press releases and general statements. So far there had been very little interest in Venice, but he knew they were waiting. Newsmen like Vince Baker, who made a career out of making the major players sweat. In fact, when Kinney had seen him the other day during the fishing fiasco, he felt sure that Baker would churn that drama into something that somehow implicated Venice of America. He just wanted to keep reporters like that away and control the news of Venice himself by feeding anecdotes to the entertainment guys. Bernhardt was a risk. He knew that. She had a reputation for speaking out or doing crazy things, so maybe that pier incident should not have come as too big a surprise (although her reputation clearly had the potential to be an asset). He just had to keep a sharper eye on things. It was a gamble he needed to take. How else could he get a star of her caliber to his place? Against his better instinct, he was willing to trust Max Klein's ability to hold the reins. But one slipup and Kinney was taking control of the whole production, and don't think for one moment that he was afraid of the reputation and brilliance of Sarah Bernhardt. The only thing that scared him was the newspapers. Not Sarah Bernhardt. Not the Catholics. Just guys like Vince Baker. Just the gutter press.

It could cost him a king's ransom to make sure the story was set straight.

She leaned against the stage, feeling the ridged edge of the floor cut against the back of her neck. A big empty house, almost tomblike. She might have been anywhere. Standing in the middle of a blank canvas while the artist mixed the colors to paint the scene. It doesn't take too long to find out that no matter how expansive and different the world, a theater stripped of life is the same everywhere. This was the lull that she detested most. The point before the stage takes form. When everybody is running around confused, as if they have never done this before, and absolutely convinced that nothing is going to work. Then they scream at one another for a while before cowering down to her to adjudicate the matter, only to have her render the same judgment: "Isn't this what I pay you for?"

She might have gone over the top with Alexandre. It is simply amazing how quickly even the most self-assured can regress into the common insecurities that overtake the room. As lead carpenter, Alexandre had constructed this set at least a thousand times now. Today he was compelled to doom. Nothing was going to work. "I don't think we can have the set done in time. The impossibilities are too large," he lamented in that hollow refrain of the amateur. Per usual, Sarah was forced to turn into mother (it didn't work out well once in its organic biological state, why would it work in this removed case?), and she had to have him explain the problem, thereby reducing the panic to levelheaded planning. "Tell me from start to finish," she had said to Alexandre, as her eyes drifted around the large hall.

"This theater is not proper for a production of this level of intimacy," he said. Nodding his head. Waiting for her reply.

"I do not know what you mean," she said. "Intimate?"

"This set is designed to be personal. As though the audience was peering through the windows of 9, rue d'Antin. But look at the size of this room." He swept his hand in a dramatic gesture. "It is as if they are looking in from the neighboring rooftop. As though we are turning the audience from members of the cast to simple gawkers. And that is not what you wanted. From the start that is not what you have wanted."

The trembling panic in his voice was becoming annoying. "What are your suggestions?" she asked, trying to calm down the almost girlish frenzy.

"I am lost, Madame Bernhardt."

"Are you paid to be lost?"

"I mean in options. I suppose that we could construct a thrust stage. Then at least you can carry your blocking out into the audience. Just bring the stage out to them."

He was talking like an idiot now. But at least a calmer, slightly more rational idiot. "And how long would that take?"

He thought for a moment. "Provided we get the supplies, I think by the end of the day tomorrow. Assuming we can get the wood easily."

"Then that leaves one day to reconfigure the design to meet your requirements?"

"I suppose that is right. And we may need to make a rake stage to give the thrust some dimension. But, yes, that would leave about a day. You are right, Madame."

"And then, Alexandre, you are suggesting that that allows one more half day for the actors to readjust their blocking to accommodate your new stage."

"That is what I am saying."

She supposed that all men innately wanted to be mothered. That they wanted the women in their lives to listen, to hold, and ultimately to scold them. That in fact they were incapable of making decisions and acting without brooding, before the conciliatory nuzzle at the maternal bosom. She imagined that at some point it would become tiresome for the men, because god knows it was for the women. But nevertheless, she gave Alexandre what he wanted when she told him he was being foolish. "You think that this production is one that can just be manipulated and twisted to fit your convenience and vision of the day? Do you think that Renoir just alters his paintings because the room that they happen to be hanging in isn't the perfect dimension? You think he just adds an extra foot to the bottoms, or adds a slight triangle off to the sides for that salon? That that is the only way for him to ensure that his audience has the proper experience."

Alexandre started to turn away out of instinct, not rebellion.

"You cannot expect the actors to restage the entire production based on the house that we are in. There are subtleties to each movement. Purpose behind each footstep. It's not a matter of moving the masking tape a few feet in this direction or that direction. Every inch has motive. Every inch has emotion. Every inch retells the story."

And now that his head had significantly hung low, she came back with calming, reassuring words. (Isn't that what he expects Mommy to do?) "Trust me and the actors. If the fourth wall is deeper, then we will have to make the intimacy of our lives that much louder. Trust that we will not drown in this giant bubble, but rather that we will fill it. Don't be such a man, Alexandre—where you have to knock things down all the time to have them make sense to you."

He nodded without any more words and walked away,

looking partially relieved and partly ashamed. And for Sarah, she wondered if there was any part of her life outside the privacy of her hotel room when she didn't have to act (as though her conviction to the current performance could be that strong). Everybody saw her in whatever roles suited their needs: from the true professionals to the conductor tearing her train tickets, to the man trying to run his tongue along her thighs. Shakespeare was right when he said that all the world was a stage. A real performance for the ages at all times.

Out of the corner of her eye, she saw Kinney at the back of the house watching the whole thing. Hands on his hips, his expression loaded with sternness and judgment. There is nothing worse than a promoter that wants to be involved. They all try to sculpt art out of wadded paper bills. Then Max walked up to Kinney, and she couldn't even look. She paced the stage back and forth, looking up into the rafters.

Waiting.

Waiting.

Waiting for what?

She didn't notice Max until she felt the gentle touch of his fingers against her forearm. He had a woman's hand. Long, delicate fingers, slender from the base to the tips, that moved with a detached fluidity, with a grip that could only tease and never spank. She turned around with a slight degree of irritation, hoping that he had come to offer a furlough from this ridiculousness of pre-preshow anxieties. "Things are looking good" was all he said.

"Don't start with me, Molly. You know that I love you too much for what I could possibly say. But for now, I can give you a whole list of things you can address to free me from the nonsense. Like you can ask Ibé why he is being so insolent about not having a proper dressing room. He has screamed at me twice: once that the wigs will be visible behind the masking, and twice that he is being set up beside a makeup station and that the pancake bases and cream blushes will ruin his wigs. *My* wigs, he pointed to me. Do you agree that I should not have to put up with this?"

"They are your crew."

"As only you could say to me. But I thought that I had hired a professional entourage, not a contingent of panicky schoolchildren. *His* wigs. And all of this seems like idiocy and distractions until we can get to the heart of the play, Molly. We are just hammering away. Pretending that all is normal. The truth is that we don't have a play here anymore, Molly. We have a set and script filled with lines. And a Marguerite that nobody knows anymore. Once more, I have to be forced to manage all this childish behavior."

Max held on to Sarah's forearm, gently releasing his grip, and turning it to a mannered stroke. Like that of an old matron with her favored but finicky pussycat. "You more than anybody know that it is part of the art of theater," he said. "The panic is the basis of the nervous energy that instills the emotion into the performance. From the stagehands' frenzy about the mechanics to your irritation. It is as much about the play as the final production. You understand as well as I do that the day that this is all laissez-faire is the day when we put on the flattest show ever played."

"This seems like excrement. Not excitement. Perhaps it is no longer my reading of the play. Maybe it is just that I am too old, Molly."

"Let's not talk of old today. We'll run through the play tonight to calm all fears and concerns of this strange house.

And then later you and I will cozy up in your room and try to find the soul of Marguerite Gautier. You heard Kinney, the initial troubles are behind us. Now we just go ahead. Like one, two, three." He tapped her arm in cadence. "One-two-three."

"You are such a molly's Molly," she said. He could manage to make light out of anything, and it could not ever occur to him that feeling old and useless was more than the end effect of a crisis. For Max, depressive states were symptomatic reactions to situations easily rectified. Problem. Sad. Fixed. One-two-three. It will devastate him when he finds out how real she is. More real than he could possibly ever have imagined.

"Just a little while longer?" he asked.

"You will pardon me if I'm too exhausted for this."

There were no words. She truly was exhausted and not just delivering a dramatic exit line to extinguish the conversation. She could not believe that Max wouldn't see it in her eyes. That there was almost a refusal to look with any depth, like looking into an eclipse, afraid that what he sees may blind him. It was as if he thought he had to stand guard for both of them, knowing that one sign of weakness, one inkling of surrender, would permanently drop the curtain. So maybe Max wasn't so unaware of the crisis that was igniting her. He was merely trying to smother it, through feigned ignorance and disbelief.

"Molly," she said, "I really don't need to be here right now. They will figure it out better without me here."

"Maybe you are right. You can go to your car to rest for a little while until we need you."

"My railcar is here?" She smiled.

"Let me just tell Kinney that I am going to walk you out there. He's like a chessmaster patiently waiting for one errant move."

"You don't need to walk me there."

"But I have the key."

"I can certainly hold a key, Molly. What, are you going to lock me in there? Cage in the unpredictable lioness?"

Max's face softened from Max Klein, international manager for the world's greatest star, to Molly, the lost tragic little gay boy who found a home in the world of the diva whom he worshipped, the envy of the lost little gay boy world. His eyes squinted in a genuine smile, sending out little lines that betrayed his age to his boyish demeanor, but nevertheless looked as innocent and scared and hopeful as the day she first met him. And in that moment she wanted to forget Abbot Kinney's theater in the middle of nowhere, forget that barn that needed to be miraculously reconfigured to the intimacy of the Parisian stage (for God's sake, the place was large enough to hold all of Paris), allow the musty, moldy smell that had seeped into every slat of wood from the moist air to leave her senses, and just hold Molly like she had in the early days. When a simple eye-to-eye signal had sparked an all-day ticket for mayhem and laughter and reckless indecision, one that instantly took their seriousness of the theater out for a few breathing hours. It seemed like they were living more before they tried to get serious about living. And she really had fallen in love with him in a way that nobody could understand. It was so much deeper than anything else that she had ever really known in her life because it was a love based on pure selfless trust. The church hadn't offered her that successfully. Nor acting. Not her family. Nor her romances. Only her Molly. He had no motives. No ambitions toward something greater. Only pure, exonerated love for the passion that was her soul. But like most relationships, it seemed to have turned to business and the management of life. Keeping track of schedules.

Money. Futures. Policing each other. And only occasionally could it be broken up with a quiet intimate dinner, but even then the business of the relationship slowly seeped in. They were a partnership now. Overtaken by comfort and routine. Something that even their past respective romances hadn't been able to destroy.

"Please walk me to my railcar, Molly," she said. "I can't imagine going there without you."

Max reached down to take her hand. There were grunts and moans from the crew as they lifted a wall of painted bricks and cutout windows to stage left. And high up in the grid another pair of men were tying down the pulleys that would raise the interior of Marguerite's anteroom, and lower the walls of the country house in Bougival. The hammers banged away, shooting disjointed echoes across the hall like ricocheting gun blasts. Nails were held in waiting between teeth. Men hovered with hands on their hips. An occasional melody hummed from an indecipherable corner of the room that suddenly stopped and then was picked up unconsciously from another corner of the house. It all worked in a mechanical rhythm like the most sophisticated piece of machinery the age could offer. All coming together beautifully, as do the actors onstage.

Max forgot to tell Kinney where they were going. They walked right out of the theater. Temporarily two young lovers.

IT WAS DARK INSIDE THE RAILCAR. The plush black curtains, faded velvet stained purplish by dust streaks, were pulled tight, allowing only a sliver of light to slice through the part in the middle, leaving a dirty darkness. The twenty-five-by-ten-foot container smelled like it had been locked up tight for the past three days, which it had. The normally nondescript smells that flavored the essence of the furnishings emanated their own brand of staleness when left alone. The scent of inertia bled from lack of breath in the cluttered single room. Max once referred to it as an abandoned whorehouse, and another time as a gypsy fortune-teller's lair. A long, wide bed blocked off the back, fluffed up by a rumpled comforter with random brown stains that splattered out like haphazard sunrays, and bordered by a heap of threadbare pillows covered in what once had been the finest spun cotton. Behind it hung bright cherry wainscoting that was more funereal than royal. Along the right side sat a red velvet provincial couch, its richly cherry-colored legs standing like lazy soldiers on duty, buttressed against a rosewood table that held a Chinese vase and a Saxe statuette. Opposite it was a vanity with the mirror expanding up and wide in an ornate frame, carelessly brushed white more than once (its master carver surely would be horrified to see his detailed craft mauled by thick brushstrokes). The desktop was littered with small bottles of perfume made of cut glass and with silver tops, surrounded by jars of makeup and pills and brushes and clips and combs and traces of forgotten jewelry.

Sitting above the couch was the press photo of her taken in her infamous coffin some years back, placed perfectly so that it reflected in the center of the mirror. Her eyes seductively closed, arms crossed, and her lips drawn apart partly in defiance and partly in childish restraint, under the light of a single candle, while near the bottom of the casket was the inscription *Quand Même*, the reminder that said she had fought against all odds. She loved that picture most. Her initial attraction had been to its smugness and defiance. How in a tongue-in-cheek manner she had managed to pooh-pooh

the mores of the lingering reactionary class that fought tooth
and nail to preserve the values of what they alone claimed
as a stranglehold on decency. They perceived all change as a
threat, and especially art that challenged thought, as opposed
to merely memorializing. And as though insurgencies such as
the French Revolution had never happened, these conservative
moles turned their tiny little voices into megaphone thunder,
declaring with undying conviction what was right for the rest
of the world. Vocalized by currency and the politicians that
they owned. Then imagine being a woman who challenges
them. One who does not fear her femininity and actually bends
and mutates it into hundreds of different forms that dare
the country and then the world to think and reconsider. And
sometimes it doesn't matter that she has to take a man's form
or adopt a whore's body or lash with a revolutionary's tongue,
because that is her calling. And then the little moles start to
scamper back and forth nervously, crisscrossing, banging into
one another, trying to get the machinery in an order that will
at the very least shape this woman into something a little more
docile and respectable—and, at the minimum, shut that bitch
up! So they try to slander. Call for the death of this immoral
insurgence. And what do they get?—Sarah Bernhardt posed
in a casket. The slight grin on her face rising between two lips
that have just told them to fuck off. And what the moles have
failed to understand is the will of the people, and how much
they love their actress. So when she poses in that casket, the
entire new world bursts out a collective laugh that rocks the
moles so hard that their little cave tunnels quake, eventually
burying them in old unnutritious soil, dedicated to wiping
the grin off that casket woman's face so that they can stand
back on the top of the mountain. All these years later the

picture is still hanging, that perfect frontier between drama and defiance. Looking back down on her as a reminder of what making art is truly about. And oddly enough she did not recognize that patron saint of freedom of thought as herself. In fact, when Sarah first entered the railcar after bidding Max a quick farewell, she collapsed onto the couch and looked up at the picture with admiration. Almost speaking aloud to it for guidance and support. Calling on herself to find the same strength that the woman in the picture had.

Sarah loved the railcar for its comfort. It smelled of Paris. The sooty air. Remnants of perfume bouquets. Sweet butter caked into the furniture. And the spilled red wine stains hidden by the matching burgundy carpet and well-traveled ashtrays smelled of the breath of every Frenchman she had ever loved. This was her home. A place to go when the pressure became too much. When she needed a warm comforting bosom to cuddle into. And each time she entered the railcar it seemed like she fell to that couch and let out a sigh that blew a deep breath from within her, extricating all the posture and strength and image and grandness that inflated the tiny being of Henriette-Rosine Bernard into the larger-than-life Sarah Bernhardt. And she could almost see the breath coming out of her, as though it had its own form, a perfect cylinder colored chalky gray with a faint light in the middle, bellowing out of her mouth and then dissipating over the room in millions of crystalline shards that floated down lone and powerless. Then she would lay her head into her hands and cry. Sometimes for an hour straight. Sometimes less. Letting the warm tears stream down her cheek, mixing with the mucus that she didn't bother to try to inhale. The gluey composite ran over her lips and sometimes her tongue, which made her cry even harder because she knew that she was tasting something real, that there was indeed flesh and bones sculpting this world.

BY LATE AFTERNOON, Vince Baker rode the red car into downtown Los Angeles. He figured that C. C. Brown's might not be the worst place to go. He could deal with Fay's petulance, certainly more than he could with Scott's hot-breath demands for the latest installment on the Bernhardt story.

Once he had sat down, he thought about wanting to get back on his Hollywood piece—one that oddly enough also had involved Bishop Conaty. The newly growing Hollywood was a village whose confused identity was the soul of its intrigue. A locale that Bishop Conaty was desperate to preserve. A place torn between old-fashioned morality and innovation. The very collision of mores and new aesthetics. It was only last year that the city had voted to keep liquor out, in response to the area becoming a magnet for decadence. Bernhardt would love this tidbit for the irony: Bishop Conaty, sensing the need to protect the piety of Hollywood, bought the Sisters of the Immaculate Heart in east Hollywood and founded a new academy and novitiate of the sisterhood. Baker had interviewed the bishop while he politicked for his new academy (one that did not come cheap at $10,000), and Conaty had exclaimed joy at announcing the news that the liquor ban had passed with a vote of 113–96. The bishop never even considered that there were more than 700 people who lived there, and a total vote of 209 was barely more than a quarter of the population. As a reporter, all the vote told Baker was that there were only 113 people that the Los Angeles liquor industry could pay off to vote in their favor. After that, only 96 people really cared either way.

Baker spotted a destitute man who faced backward near the front of the car. The bum's feet tapped alternate rhythms while his fingers drummed on his knees. His empty irises darted side to side. At one point they caught Baker's, before leaping away at the exact moment of recognition. The man spoke to himself in a polite and respectful tone, never yelling and carrying on like some hobos can do, always keeping a reserved expression that painfully tried to hold back a dangerous smile. The man kept looking over at him. Talking. Shifting his eyes. Mumbling. Fumbling with his hands, intermingling his fingers. He then held Baker's stare for a moment and whispered loud enough for him to hear, "There is no other name under heaven given among men by which we must be saved than the name of Jesus," at which Baker laughed hysterically.

When Baker did file off the trolley at Seventh and Spring, the streets felt eerie, as if they were keeping secrets and engaging in conspiratorial whispers behind the midafternoon curtain of the shopping and business district. The unusual number of young people strolling the sidewalks in vociferous dereliction was a clear indicator of what the real downtown was about. Not Broadway with its theaters, haberdasheries, and ladies' boutiques. In this deeper downtown, moral requisites looked like afterthoughts. Men sauntered in carnival laughter, trailed by flirtatious young women who looked liked the pen-and-ink models advertising "stylish, natty" ladies' alpaca bathing suits from $1.98 to $5.00 in the local papers.

He made his way into C. C. Brown's, "Home of the Ice Cream Sundae." Bright lights reflected off the spotless white tiled floor. The counter was crowded with young girls set sidesaddle on the black cushioned stools while their overattentive dates stood beside them, each suitor competitively focused on attracting the attention of the lone waitress or ice cream jerk to fulfill his girl's wishes, straddling the line between chivalry and puppy dog-ness. Traces of ammonia fumes rose from the floor in battle with the pungency of hours-old spilt ice cream and the sweaty anticipation of love. It was loud inside the place. Reams of laughter unrolled in stark contrast to the funereal utterances of the formal downtown establishments like Al Levy's. People were alive in C. C. Brown's. It was the Los Angeles of possibility. This area was not about broken promises or ambivalent possibilities. It was about here. About now. Where yesterday was gone and there was no tomorrow. It was not about dreaming, but about living dreams. All as long as you stayed within its confines and didn't accidentally cross your way into Chinatown. Baker figured that after the good bishop saved Hollywood, he would surely press his efforts in this direction and into the seediness of the Chinese district. The subject had vaguely come up in Baker's interview with the bishop, his expression practically cracking into four distinct pieces and slithering off his face when he had said the word *Chinatown*, as if it were code for *hell*. Although the bishop's reaction had hardly registered with Baker during that interview, it should have told him in five words or less everything he needed to know about Conaty. In retrospect he could have predicted the Sarah Bernhardt decency boycott the moment he walked into the bishop's rancid-smelling office.

Fay immediately made her way over to the table, the water pitcher in hand. Her expression was equal parts confusion and domain. "Why I'm surprised to see you here," she said, focusing her stare solely on Baker.

He leaned in to try to whisper. "I am here to get away from work is all."

Fay stepped back, the water pitcher shaking in her hand. "Vince Baker," she said.

No reporter likes to have his name blurted out in public, it's like hanging a fly strip over roadkill on a hot day. Baker leaned in closer, hoping to stifle her volume. He could smell her breath. Two-hour-old cigarette smoke, flat coffee, and the unsuccessful blanket of something minty. She still smelled of this morning, with yesterday's tastes settled into a ubiquitously sensuous and repulsive brew. "Jesus Christ, Fay."

Fay's nose winced as she forced her eyes to comply with her smile. The almost sandy perfection of her hair was pulled back and pinned to her head with just three symmetrical but renegade strands touching her neck. Her pure blue eyes that radiated simplicity and honesty with a real-world edge looked as though they would explode in either tears or rage.

Baker sighed as he leaned back in his chair. The booze, the lack of sleep, and the adrenaline push were all starting to catch up. At another moment he might have panicked, but at this particular instance, in the brightly lit hub of L.A. life, where careless youth seemed to live out an infinite eternity, he just looked at her and said she should relax. It really was just work.

Fay placed the water pitcher on the table. "Boy, oh boy. I am really touched. You know how to melt a girl's heart." She looked at him, a smile half-broken, with a hand on her hip. Her eyes darted over the slowly refilling room. "I better get back to the floor. And you better get to work." She turned and walked away.

The volume inside C. C. Brown's began to rise, scored by the teenage girls' high-pitched screams of recognition and the slurring growl of their male escorts, occasionally punctuated by imitation country club laughter. The shrill was nearly unbearable. The second wave of the afternoon washed in on the coattails of barely contained hormones, a gut-wrenching glimpse of the future, and a sad reminder of the past in which the ghosts of their parents spooked loud and clear. The curse was in getting older. Give or take the notion of predisposition, there wasn't a kid on this earth who wasn't open to new ideas, where ideology and politics and pedagogy and ethics don't cloud every perception. But with each year, judgments begin to fog those ideals until the child begins to see the world through one of the four or so available sets of adult perceptions. It is only the rare ones, the cracks in the gene pool, who break through. Someone, it occurred to him, like Sarah Bernhardt.

Baker left C. C. Brown's, having escaped Fay's petulant glare reflected in the copper kettles that cooked the chocolate sauce. He caught the red car back home, with a plan for an all-day stop at Willie's, sure to escape whatever chase Fay might be calculating. He wished he could hide out all week. Scott was not going to let up on him until he handed in a Bernhardt piece. And he still had no strategy. By tomorrow, he supposed, he would have to take a ride out to Venice. Hoping he could catch some story.

Baker arrived back at his Pico apartment at five minutes before eleven, if his clock was to be trusted. He lit the room, still shadowed in meticulously placed clutter. The bed was tossed by rumpled sheets that had been kicked in the corner from last night's tryst. He thought about Bernhardt. He had not seen her up close. But from the distance on the pier, her eyes had looked weighted down in exhaustion, but her shoulders poised in pride. He supposed he had to admit that there was something intriguing about her. The sun's golden glow traced the edges of her form, but still he hardly saw her elevated to a level of immortality, something unearthly akin to the progeny of Leda and Zeus as the Scotts of the world would have you believe.

Baker sat in his overstuffed chair, upholstered in a mysterious green fabric that was fraying in such a way that it resembled a shedding dog. The seat was cluttered with tossed clothes. Some had been partially folded and appeared to have been forgotten. He reached down and pinched a handful of T-shirts and trousers, and then quickly flung them onto a pile of boxes. He wondered what he might eventually say to her, and if she would even talk with him. He would be forced by professional integrity to identify himself as a reporter, and she undoubtedly would scream bloody murder for her people to get him the hell out of there. He had to be careful about making eye contact with Bernhardt. He could tell she was the type who had a spell. The kind of hold that would take you prisoner, locked into the cell of her world, where you quickly relinquished all your strength and stature. Sublimated by her power. When she said *dance*, you danced.

He stayed in his chair into the early morning, listening to a light rumble of thunder that sounded as natural as a distant train. Then he heard the beginning of the rain. Large, heavy drops that fell dumbly down, splattering against the concrete with the first coating of wet. The rain began to scratch against his window with paw print remnants, and then pick up into the fast but steady rhythms of Mexican maracas. He kept his eyes closed while he listened. The rain was cleansing. Reassuring. Today was being whitewashed, and tomorrow morning when he finally did go outside, Los Angeles would sparkle. The bushes would glisten green. Sparkling lawns. The leaves twinkling off the trees. It would be the city of angels.

And he would remember the power of being here. The place where anybody can make anything possible.

Sarah Bernhardt kept crossing his mind. A lot, considering that he didn't really care about her. He wasn't thrilled with having to lower himself to talk with her. But he was curious to see her again. He would catch some story tomorrow.

He kept his eyes closed. And listened to the rain.

THE RAILCAR WAS STILL and dark, and though tightly sealed, the barks of seagulls and the low groans of thunder rumbled throughout the train's narrow passage as though part of the atmosphere.

She dropped her head back and began to hum "Sur le Pont d'Avignon." The childhood song rarely came into her head. Often she would try to summon it during insomniac nights, but the simple melody could never compete with the thundering thoughts that banged through her mind. It was only the rare times like these when the lyrics and melody just appeared free and uncluttered. When all became pure, and she heard her mother's sweet voice singing peacefully and calmly of dancing on the old bridge of Avignon. *Sur le pont d'Avignon / Tout le monde y danse, danse.* Mama's golden hair gleaming in the shadows. Sweet butter on her breath. Henriette-Rosine would be resting her head on a crushed feather pillow, lying on a mattress that was as secure as the wood frame that supported it. Four years old. In Paris. Neuilly on the banks of the Seine. Those were the nights before Mama left. Before she disappeared into travels for more than two years. When Henriette-Rosine still believed her father was working in China and would return any day. Before she found herself living alone with the family nurse in a windowless room at 65, rue de Provence, waiting for her mother to return. When all was still perfect. All was still hopeful. A voice of the universe telling her that all the world dances around. *Sur le pont d'Avignon / Tout le monde y danse, danse / Sur le pont d'Avignon / Tout le monde y danse en rond.*

She stopped humming for a moment, and loosed a content, sleep-filled sigh.

She leaned her head back and began to hum again.

Sur le pont d'Avignon / Tout le monde y danse, danse.

Henriette-Rosine was ready to go to sleep. She closed her eyes. The side of her face turned against the softened upholstery.

Sur le pont d'Avignon / Tout le monde y danse en rond.

The smell of sweet butter washed over her.

CHAPTER FIVE
May 17, 1906

MAX thought she looked at peace in the morning
light. Her body in a deep slumber, something that eluded her
almost every night since she had arrived in America. Now she
slept soundly. Tucked into the railcar bed, lying on her back
with her head propped up by a pillow set just below her neck.
To some she might have looked like a perfect specimen at a
viewing. He sat down next to her and stroked her hair. He froze
when she had startled for a moment, twitching her head and
making mumbling half-words. There were all those stories about
waking people from sleepwalking, and how they never again
recovered from the disorientation. Shocked into mental illness,
permanently placed in a state of anxious melancholia. Max
felt the warmth of her breath cross his cheek. It had floated
with dandelion ease, stopping just before his skin in pure
intoxication.

Kinney had arranged a brunch with certain patrons of the area. They had paid charitable prices for the front-row seats and had been promised an intimate brunch with the star. Although it was not for another hour and a half, Max needed to wake her. Most of her clothes, and the comfort of her bath, were in her room at the King George. She was not one who rose quickly in the morning, nor was she especially brisk with things like changing locations.

"You have come to kidnap me." Her voice was gravelly. Her eyes only half open. She crossed her arms over her chest in a dead man's pose and looked up at the ceiling. The blankets pushed down heavy on her, cocooning her in safety.

"I wish I could let you sleep all day," Max said.

She lifted her right arm up and beckoned him with her hand. "Come here. You deserve to have comfort."

"That's all right." He shook his head. "I'm fine."

"Ridiculous. Come keep warm under the covers. We can watch the ceiling together."

Max was the kind of man who lifted the world on his shoulders for show, and then forgot it was there. In such desperate allegiance to clocks and schedules. He had the strength to mow down the threats, yet when he looked in the mirror, he was still the same scared little boy who first peeked out from between his mother's legs to see the world. He didn't move, just maintained his stance over the bed.

"Let's just hide all day here," she said. "Keep the covers on and the curtains drawn. And we can read dialogue. We can pick a play that we have never read together and recite it for an audience of nobody other than ourselves. Then when we exhaust that, we can solve the mystery of Marguerite Gautier."

Max grinned and told her that he wished that they could

do that (and the truth was that he really did wish that they could do that), but it seemed like years had passed since their schedules had ever allowed for that kind of recreation. "I really am sorry," he said. "But we have the Patrons' Brunch."

"Patrons' Brunch?"

"Yes, I told you. It is on your itinerary."

"It is just the way you say it: *Patrons' Brunch* . . . Is that your term?"

"Well, that is how Kinney has billed it."

"Can we please refrain from using his antiseptic vernacular. It is not only distasteful, but it is also in contradiction to the whole notion of what we are about. We produce art to give people a vehicle by which they can view the world in new ways—not limited jingoistic phrases that one can take comfort in without thinking."

"Sarah, I will call it whatever you prefer."

"No. Call it what *you* prefer. That is my point."

"What if I prefer 'Patrons' Brunch'?"

She kicked the covers up and off, and then sat up. "You know, Molly, you are truly more effective than a two-bell alarm clock."

"Come then," he said.

Sarah sat on the edge of the bed. She braced her forehead in her palms. And for one brief moment, Max saw her as different from the Sarah that they had worked to preserve in reputation and memory. Almost as ordinary. Her unwashed face was stripped of makeup, other than black lines that traced her eyes. Shoulders stooped in resignation and wear. And she stared off as if there were no thoughts in her head. Then she dropped her hands to look back at him with a twinkle that was equal parts innocence, power, malice, and instability. He smiled for the

Sarah that again he recognized. She dropped back onto the bed and kicked her feet up in the air. "Please tell them thank you, but I will have to decline."

"I am afraid that that is not an option."

She pouted out a blast of breath. "Then you can go in my place. I can sign some pictures now. You'll bring them. And then you apologize for my current condition, of which they won't even question because they will be certain that I must have at least one, and you can answer the questions. You have heard them all a thousand times before, and certainly you must have the quips and stories committed to memory by this point in our partnership."

"I am flattered by your confidence, but this is not negotiable. Part of the contract. Plus we are never in a position to turn down money."

"And then when do you expect that we can discuss the play? We are opening tomorrow, and it is still in chaos."

"The play is not in chaos. Last night's run-through was smooth. The set is working. The cast is comfortable. The only issue is the sudden change in your relationship to your character. Frankly, that is something for you to work out with me. Not to throw the entire company into disarray with."

"Again, it is clear how little you know about acting."

"But I do know about the theater."

"And when do we meet to discuss these changes? We haven't shared more than one or two serious sentences about it. You keep telling me we will get to it, but something else of greater importance manages to take precedence. And now it is a brunch that is sure to last half the day. Then you will have to attend to your new boyfriend Kinney, and then another silly run-through, and soon it's dinner. And you will say that we should discuss the matter after dinner. So where does that leave us with tomorrow being opening night? What room does that leave for changes? You don't think that I can ask the actors to rethink their entire motivations three hours before curtain. It's ridiculous enough to bring it up to them with only one day in advance."

"Sarah, why don't you just play Marguerite as you have always played her—for now. We can look at revamping the production once we have some time. When we are back in Paris."

"And act a part that I don't feel? I might as well quit."

"I promise we will make time today to discuss this."

"You will put that on the itinerary?"

"Once we are back at the hotel, yes."

"Because I cannot perform as Sarah Bernhardt reciting the lines of Dumas's Marguerite."

"I know."

"I can only go on if I am Marguerite."

She straightened herself into a firm posture. Patted her hair into place. Tugged down on her dress and then grabbed the material at the hips to center it. She arched her chin up slightly, as the photographers always tried to suggest. Shoulders rolled back. A long breath to expand the lungs. "I wish you were a playwright who could write me out of this scene," she grumbled. Then she knocked her knuckles twice against the warm door for luck, before opening it. She stood in the doorway, a one-dimensional die-cut of radiance pasted between the deep blue sky and the haunted red train. Like a spirit revealing itself to the day.

Off to the Patrons' Brunch.

Time to be Sarah Bernhardt.

Vince Baker sat inside the King George Hotel lobby, keenly aware of how different the air felt, trapped and rarefied. He had been camped for about an hour, staking out the place. He still had no real objective other than to see her. It had been twice now that he had been in her presence, and each time he had the strange feeling that the distance made him understand her a little more. Soon he was going to be forced to have to talk with her (although he worried her allure might seduce him into a dumb state, one that extended beyond the physiology of the mouth, more like a brain that temporarily lost its ability to form thoughts). He wasn't scared of her. But he did recognize her ability to reshape charisma into control. She would probably want to speak with him once she was told that it was his name on the article that publicly flogged her. She would want to set the record straight. They all do. He still needed to figure out what he would say to her. And be able to say it.

Bernhardt pressed through the lobby doors in a dramatic fashion that was likely her calling card. All eyes instantly leaped toward her. Baker presumed this as normal. She was trailed close behind by the escort from the other night who at once appeared controlled and hurried. She looked slightly disheveled. Her hair, which both times before always seemed on the edge of kempt now sprang out as though unsuccessfully matted by tap water and a comb. Her dress appeared a bit wrinkled, as almost an elegant housedress, but certainly not what one would imagine her to be seen wearing in public. And perhaps that was the very reason that her escort guided her quickly through a small crowd that was as eager to get a glimpse of her as she was to see them. He took her right into the stairwell and effectively locked her in, before swinging open the door with the gracious hands of a politician on a whistle-stop to announce, "Thank you for coming. I am sorry to be so brief, but Madame needs her rest." And the small crowd, an equal mix of old and young, accepted this proclamation, not for one moment questioning why the ingenue would need to rest so early in the morning.

Baker watched the group disperse and noticed a slight change in their demeanors. It was as if they walked a little taller, somehow ingesting her confidence and charisma by proxy. Maybe this is the allure of the autograph. It is more than obtaining proof or having a keepsake, and even beyond establishing connection—it is removing part of that person, a graft, and infusing it into your own system, the momentary feeling that you are one and the same.

In an odd way Baker felt it too. He had the same sense of empowerment from having witnessed something historic, where your place in the world quickly feels more relevant. Your feet know what it is like to fall in the trail of greatness. And as with the autograph, you completely rise to a new level. Baker felt ready to talk with her. A sit-down interview to try to understand the illusion of her power. How this petite old French women whose vocation was in repeating words from a playwright's hand could cause such an upheaval.

He stepped up to the desk and leaned over, bracing himself by the elbows. Eye to eye with the head clerk. "Can you please direct me to Sarah Bernhardt's room?" he said, cutting off the salutation.

The clerk coughed into his fist. "You understand that I cannot give out that information."

"I'm a reporter from the *Los Angeles Herald*. Vince Baker. I only wish to interview her."

"I am not allowed to." His voice nearly broke.

Baker was not accustomed to encountering this type of situation. His credentials and reputation usually gave him a free pass through any door, from the top-floor office suite to the mistressed boudoirs. "How about a message to her, then." He reached for a pencil in his coat. "Have some paper, please?"

The clerk's lips barely moved, uttering something inaudible.

"There a problem here?"

"I just don't know if I should be bothering her."

"Let me tell you something"—he leaned forward to read the clerk's nametag—"Dolph. You don't think Miss Bernhardt finding out that she missed a chance for an interview with the *Herald* will cause some problems? She's a celebrity. That's what they live for. And I am especially guessing that you don't want to read in the article that Bernhardt was not available for comment because old Dolph at the King George Hotel refused to pass the request along. Actually, I imagine that you don't want Abbot Kinney reading that either."

Dolph's complexion turned white, with a thin but visible band of sweat banding his forehead.

"Well?" Baker spoke. This time sounding more impatient.

"I suppose there is no harm in delivering a message."

Dolph disappeared for several minutes, leaving Baker strangely alone in the lobby. The room was deserted as if the victim of an evacuation. It crossed his mind that he had missed some crucial piece of information while sparring with Dolph. After a time measured by breaths, a collection of couples passed through the lobby into the restaurant. They were paired by gender. Men set the pace with hands dug into their pockets, their brows furrowed as they nodded in conspiracy, trailed by the women who spoke in hushed voices, trying to smolder smiles that their husbands would view as treasonous.

In procession, Bernhardt and her escort shortly followed behind. She was dolled now, walking a brisk stride as though the barrel of a pistol were set deep in her kidneys. Rounding out the parade was Dolph who, out of breath, said to Baker, "Madame Bernhardt says that she will meet with you at one o'clock."

THREE WAITERS WERE POSTURED patiently, standing at military arms upon the guests' arrival, hands at their sides, shoulders squared back, and chins subtly arched toward the ceiling. It was Kinney's private dining room at the hotel. It had a certain genuine elegance that was hard to find fault with. The other guests were already seated when Sarah and Max arrived. The white-coated waiters took over, one guiding them to the table while the other two were dispensed back to the kitchen to begin relaying silver-trayed meals.

The dynamic was fairly simple. Abbot Kinney sat on one side of the table, his big hands resting on the white linen, interlacing his fingers that looked too small for those hands, while the two thumbs rubbed gently against each other. And Sarah sat opposite him. Her posture erect and her face stern and serious, pretending to be listening and attentive to all his stories as her mind drifted in and out. While at the end of the table, seated directly center, Max Klein drummed his foot nervously against the floor, accidentally clanking his fork against the china plate more than once, clearly in terror that this intimately confined setting had the potential to explode at any moment. The patrons lined the table. They sat man, woman, man, woman (although it might have made better sense to stack one side with women, and the other with men, as most couples did not engage with each other, instead they leaned and arced behind the chair backs when private discourse took precedence).

Kinney took painstaking care in introducing each member of the table to Sarah. He told their names, where their families came from, the husband's line of work, and a lengthy reading of their commitment to the arts that read more like a curriculum vitae than a brunch introduction. When he was finished, Kinney turned to Max and added, "This is Maxwell Klein, Madame's manager and confidant." Then he turned from Max as quickly.

The waiters never broke a sweat. Sarah noticed that. They performed in their perfectly executed tandem, never betraying the anxiety or stress of transporting food that was prepared with a chef's vision. Careful not to disrupt the presentation and not to lose the proper serving temperature of the meals, while keeping a shadowed presence inside the room, on the unenviable cusp of having to be readily engaged and as impassive as the walls. She was struck by their professionalism. Their drive for perfection. And she wondered what instilled this ethic. Surely there was not enough money to engender this level of commitment, nor (and even more baffling) was there an audience to applaud their efforts. At best they might be palmed a nice gratuity at the end of the evening, followed by a concessionary elitist comment such as, *The service was quite nice tonight.* But maybe that was enough. Maybe recognition, even in its barest most questionable form, was the motivation for excellence. She was thinking about that when Kinney asked if there was a problem with the food. She just wasn't very hungry, she told him, half-expecting him to order the waiters to find some other accommodations. Mostly though, she was not hungry from boredom.

To Sarah's right sat a woman with a slight frame. She wore her blond hair twisted and pinned to the back of her head with the sides shaped like cones. Her cheeks puffed out uncomfortably, as though she was the victim of a cultural melancholia only cured by food (and clearly not her husband's money). She wore a wedding ring with a slim silver band, almost invisible, but on top sat a fat diamond that vied for balance each time she moved a finger. She was the wife of Dr. Cornelius Michaels (none of the women seemed to have their own names), descendants of Scots, and the major funders behind the growth of the county art museum. (Or was she Mrs. Michael Connors of Prussian descent, primary funder of the ballet expansion?) She turned to Sarah and said that timeless expression: "I can't tell you what an honor this is."

Sarah nodded and smiled, whispering, "*Merci.*"

"I am so delighted to see *Camille* tomorrow night. It has been a dream of mine to see you in that role."

"I have always wondered why it is called that in America?"

"I am sorry?"

"Why do you think they call it *Camille*? That is not the name of the play."

A few of the men coughed.

"It is called *La Dame aux Camélias.*"

"Perhaps," one of the men offered (Dr. Simon, England, Sculpture?), "it has been translated because of our clumsy American tongues."

"But it translates to *Lady of the Camellias.* A reference to Marguerite always buying the flowers."

"Well, you know we Americans like things compact and succinct," said Dr. Simon, laughing.

"I find it strange," Sarah said. She took a small bite and

then chased it with a sip of champagne. "Does *Camille* even mean anything?"

"A name," Mrs. Michaels said. "In fact, my sister is named Camille."

"How very interesting."

Mrs. Michaels continued. "Again, I cannot express how much I am looking forward to watching your performance in *La Dame*—The Lady of the Camellias."

Sarah finished her glass. "It pleases me to hear your anticipation. However, I am regretful to tell you that I will not be performing *La Dame aux Camélias* tomorrow evening. I have decided to change the show to *La Tosca*."

Max's elbow nearly slipped off the table. She saw him look to Kinney, who was strangely unaffected by the news. Then Max glared at her with a look that commanded silence. She shrugged. Normally he would break in with a *what Madame meant to say* and recast her words to his neutral agenda. But this time there was nothing that Molly could possibly do with that phrase. It was clear and precise, leaving no variance for interpretation. All he could do was sit back and nod his head. He would probably look best if he just appeared agreeable, instead of stunned and unaware.

"Well." Mrs. Michaels spoke for the table. "That is a little unorthodox, isn't it? Changing shows the day before."

"Sometimes you must go with intuition," Sarah said. "It is unfair to both the company and the audience to proceed with a performance when both have lost the emotional connection. That is when decisions need to be made."

Kinney straightened at the end of the table. The words and implications finally processing through his mind. "Indeed, it does sound a bit unorthodox."

"We are a company of professionals. And a large part of our success is based on trusting our instincts. Plus, we have been playing *La Tosca* on this tour already. We have the sets. Rehearsals have been run."

Kinney nodded, looking both surprisingly content and enthralled.

"I will be frank with all of you," Sarah stated. "You are scholars of art. If you saw me perform Marguerite Gautier tomorrow night you would be very disappointed. You would leave the theater saying to one another that while it was a pleasure to see Madame Bernhardt apply her craft, still there was something lacking. You would not be able to put your finger on it, but still you would know. So I will save the discussion in two manners. First, by changing the show, and secondly by explaining that what you recognize as lacking is the admission that I am not sure that I understand Marguerite Gautier anymore."

"What Madame means to say," (there he goes) Max said, "is that she is reenvisioning Marguerite's motivations."

Sarah smiled at him. "Sitting here with you today makes me realize that I cannot possibly continue that charade. So instead we turn to *La Tosca*. A simple woman in a complex situation. One whose tragic death is by her own hand. Her own punctuation mark to end the circumstances. Where death is honor, and her freedom is in being able to choose."

"And," Dr. Simon added, "where *Tosca* translates to *Tosca*."

Abbot Kinney was no doubt bolstered by the confidence he was seeing in the patrons. "I suppose I have little choice but to trust your vision," he said. "You must have some extra work ahead of you though, Mr. Klein."

"Indeed," Max said, trying to portray support and ease. He

nearly knocked over the champagne glass while pushing it away.

"Max is very used to me by now. Isn't that right, Max?"

With all eyes on him, he forced a smile at her as though every muscle in his face had gone dead.

"Cheers." Kinney lifted his glass. "To Madame Bernhardt . . . And to instincts."

"Rightly so," somebody said under the chattering of tinkling glass.

From that point on the brunch dissolved into side conversations with very little directed to Sarah. She was already running the changes through her mind. Reconfiguring the set. Deciding on the best course for breaking the news to Alexandre in a way that would not recall another infantile tantrum. She was not enthused about making this change, but she was relieved to be free of the burden of Marguerite Gautier. All she had to do was walk right through the doors of the Sant'Andrea della Valle church and she would become Floria Tosca.

Death for honor is much easier to grasp than death for metaphor.

And in truth this was all really a giant compromise. Because her real instinct was to walk away. Stand up and say, *I retire*. But as long as she created this diversion of changing plays, acting as though there was still purpose and reasoning, then she might possibly be able to keep pushing, giving everyone something to work for, perhaps sustaining her long enough to make it through this run, and through the rest of the tour (they needed the money, Max kept reminding). But she was truly on the verge. One stubbed toe could retire this filly for life.

Following coffee and half-eaten chocolate pastries, Kinney

pushed himself away from the table and thanked everybody for coming. It was a pleasure and joy to share such an intimate time with a true legend, as well as get to be privy to her artistic thinking in person. And, he added, he looked forward to vindicating her from those Los Angeles loudmouths in their fortress cathedral. "Call it a group effort." He smiled.

Ever the professional actor, Sarah stood up for farewells. *Warm up your voice: Le bal—Le baaaaal.* She was sorry to have to leave so soon. *Nod your head.* The brunch felt like it was still only beginning. *Minor but sincere frown.* But they must all imagine the work that must be done. The arrangements and the rearrangements. *Look over to the door and then down at your feet.* She kissed them once on each cheek and wished each person well. *Slightly forgiving posture.* As they exited toward the service stairs, she took Max's hand. One that didn't seem as if it wanted to be taken.

"I guess I need to go tell them to strike the set," Max said.

"They will be charmed by the drama of it."

"Don't forget." Max started to walk away. "You have a one o'clock with that reporter."

"Cancel, please. I do not have the energy for acting anymore."

"Mr. Baker." Dolph called over to the reporter who had been sitting patiently on the cream love seat for the better part of an hour and a half. He had seen the dilettante procession parade by at least twenty minutes ago. But he had not seen Bernhardt yet. Perhaps she had escaped up a rear exit. It being 1:36 p.m., Baker was getting a little irritated. He was usually not kept waiting. "Mr. Baker."

The clerk's voice finally caught his attention. Baker rose, ready to be directed to the guest room. "Which floor, Dolph?"

"I am sorry, Mr. Baker. But Mr. Klein has just informed me that Madame Bernhardt is not feeling well. She regrets that she must cancel the interview."

"Cancel?"

"That is what Mr. Klein said."

"Did Mr. Klein suggest a better time?"

"He said only as I have told you."

"And if I want to reschedule?"

"I am just the desk clerk."

Baker turned to walk away. He didn't offer an appreciation for the effort, nor did he offer a gratuity—something that certainly could lose an ally quickly. He stood in the center of the lobby, turning a full circle and looking for something that he wasn't sure of. He wasn't used to be being canceled on. She should be pleased that he was willing to even sit down with her, and lower himself to this kind of story. In any other circumstance, he would have sooner quit than be associated with this bullshit, but he had conceded that there was a strange seduction about her that begged many questions. Baker wasn't so irritated that she had canceled (after all sick is sick), but that he had let himself be taken in by her. He should know better than that. Every reporter knows that your subjects cannot fascinate you. It is the breakdown of objectivity. The moment that you start forgiving them their faults is the same moment when you have joined their payroll. Baker was better off covering the Hollywood expansion, water wars, railroad fights, and all the other downtown scandals. He didn't trust any of those bastards for a minute.

He walked outside and sat down on a green wooden bench,

uncertain of what to do next. Wind was blowing off the whitecaps and slapping his face with a mother's scolding. The bottom line was that he still needed to file the story. Graham Scott would be twiddling his fingers, bouncing the erasers off the desk, and yelling out to Barb every thirty minutes to find out if there was any word on Baker's article.

At that moment Vince Baker could have walked away. Not just from the story, but from the whole career altogether. It's not that any of those sonsabitches had ever held a grip on him. Doheny. Harrington. Huntington. Johnson. He had the one thing that all their money combined could not buy—a voice. They did their level best to seduce him, offering glimpses into their lives and letting him have a slight touch. They made certain that the maître d's knew him by name and treated him as though he were one of the tribe. They offered to put him on their payrolls for businesses three times removed, but he never acquiesced. His distance and comparative poverty were his strength. His upper hand. But here he was, standing alone and waiting. A good reporter doesn't usually even have a half second to turn around and adjust his Johnson. A reporter's eyes roam. They catalog. They conclude. They remember. But here in the land of Abbot Kinney, between the theater and the hotel, he suddenly understood the true deference he had with all his subjects. No matter how much you think you are smoking them out, the truth is that you are always still chasing after them. You can strut and posture as much as you like, but in the end you are ultimately left waiting for the invitation. Not much of a life to lead.

But he would have still liked to get her take on the boycott. True, the bishop and his army had relaxed, but initially they still had intended to extend the boycott into Venice.

They had hounded Baker daily, led by their little messenger, Dorothy O'Brien, who was on his back both goddamned day and night to hear her plans. She left messages at the *Herald* to say that the story was not over. A certifiable nut. Living in her solitary bungalow where the paint never peels, where for two years she's walked at least one mile every day to go to the Cathedral of our Lady of Angels, where she sometimes works as an assistant to Bishop Conaty, but more often than not is a caretaker for the church, sweeping the steps, polishing the pews, and dusting the cobwebs that are spun to the Savior's nailed feet. She goddamn told him everything. Never just said her piece and went. Finally he managed to get her off his back by telling her that if he reopened the story it would not be about the success of extricating Bernhardt, rather it would investigate how the bishop was funding the new cathedral. Apparently the threat worked, because the League of Decency had turned quickly silent. (And Baker was lucky that it stopped there, because if word had reached Scott that Baker had tossed out threats to the religious community during the cleanup of the Vienna Buffet, Baker would have been knelt down in the *Herald*'s guillotine right then and there.) Dorothy O'Brien left one last message to invite him to a small victory celebration for their most trusted parishioners and the press. That's how they are, those zealots. They come frumped up in their salt-and-pepper wool overcoats, shuffling along like they are too lonely to walk, looking helpless and slightly off, and then the next thing you know they are given a little attention and they hang on you night and day, the lunacy confirmed. Baker had elected not to go. Reporters don't celebrate the outcomes of their stories with the people involved. His regret was that he probably could have made Bernhardt's story into something.

Now he would likely hack some junk out, trying to make celebrity machinations into a newsworthy piece.

Baker decided that he would hike a nonstop trip to Willie's, and throw back a stiff one that cleansed, sanitized, and burned the Bernhardt humiliation right out of his system. He stood up and paced with the same thoughtful walk of his father, taking slow languid strides as though calculating the weight of the world, when in fact there was nothing much going on inside except the quest for solitude.

He patted his breast pocket for a smoke. Left his butts at the goddamn house. He thought about his sister Leslie still back in Phoenix and her daughter Jessie. He used to bounce Jessie on his knee. They called him Uncle Vince. He had always thought he was too young to be called *Uncle*. Jessie must be huge now. It would be okay if she called him Uncle Vince. He wouldn't mind now, he thought, considering the idea that he now was old enough to be called *Uncle*.

He was about to leave when the sound of a woman's laugh caused him to turn around. In the distance, heading over to the theater, he swore he saw Bernhardt with her escort (must be Mr. Klein). Her body swayed while she walked. Her footsteps hard and proud. A strange glow shone through the edges of her hair. If it was Bernhardt, she hardly looked the infirm that the desk clerk had made her out to be.

Baker charged back into the hotel to find that goddamn wiry Dolph and find out what was really going on. Everybody knows that you don't stand up reporters in this town with bullshit excuses.

"Mr. Baker," Dolph said. "You are back."

"I want you to go up to her room again. I want to know when she thinks she will be feeling better."

Dolph shook his head. "I just don't . . ." And the way he hung indecisively on the empty phrase convinced Baker that his suspicions had been confirmed—he had been duped. She had kept him here for close to two hours, only to feign illness in order not to talk with him. Insult upon insult. Treated him like a child by employing such novice charades. Fuck this. He was walking from this story. Walking from giving her a fair shake. He could call on Dorothy O'Brien or Thomas Conaty, and then walk away with enough quotes to spill across the page like blood. And when Bernhardt woke up and saw the story in the morning edition, she would be horrified, and again stupidly wonder what she had done to deserve this wrath. And he wasn't walking away without telling her. He asked Dolph for some paper to write down what she should expect and why. Bullshitters like her always thought they were untouchable.

Baker's hand shook while he prepared to write the letter. He thought of about ten different openings, each time dropping the lead to the paper but pulling it up quickly in dissatisfaction. His self-esteem had weighted down his judgment, and his rage began to grow in place of reason and eloquence. Finally he let the pencil write:

DEAR MADAME BERNHARDT:

I assume that you are feeling better. I came prepared for our meeting at one o'clock, but had been informed that you had taken ill and would not be receiving guests. Mr. Klein has apparently fared better, as, at the time of this writing, you seemed to have found his company along the pier.

Please forgive the attention I have given to your side of the story, in hopes of writing a balanced account of your recent controversy here. Know that I will no longer try to take your time. *Instead I will concentrate my efforts back on the bishop and his agenda.*

Au revoir, Madame Bernhardt. And one suggestion: You might consider a regular suppository if you are often as sick as you are today.

Cordially,

VINCE BAKER, The Los Angeles Herald

He should not have hastened to send the note. Read it over once or twice, and then scratched out the impertinence. Instead he folded it four times and handed it to Dolph. "Please have this sent immediately."

"Would you like me to wait for a reply?"

Baker shook his head no. And he turned around and left. With his first pure sense of direction of the day.

SARAH WAS BY NO MEANS HAPPY, even though she had been laughing while she walked toward the theater with Max. She had been imagining Alexandre's expression when Max told him to change the set. Max had done a pretty good job describing the way Alexandre's shoulders seem to puff with steam while his eyes looked as if they would leak a pair of oceans.

"You really should write for the stage," she told Max.

"I bet you say that to all the boys."

"Only those who have seen me at my worst but can still make me beautiful."

She took his arm as they ascended the steps toward the arched wooden doors. The dusk felt fresh. It settled on their cheeks.

Max pulled the door open with a certain hesitancy, cracking just enough space for them to have slipped through, but then he closed it before they entered. Perhaps he sensed the reaction that she would have when faced with the theater. That the proclamation of changing plays and the newfound life that had reinvigorated her would quickly be diminished by the realities of the production. The charming image of Alexandre's angst would easily give way to her frustration with his insolence. Or Ibé frantically combing out the new wigs while loudly complaining that a man of his reputation should not have to endure such utter unprofessionalism. It would all get to her, and the enthusiasm would reveal itself as temporary, and she would storm out of the theater, looking for some solution that would inevitably consider the positive results of a hit of opium.

But for the moment all was well. She was still smiling while picturing her lead carpenter's face.

"At least you managed to curry Kinney's support," Max said. "It could have been much worse. Especially as he does not trust us."

"He still does not trust us. But he does trust his patrons' reactions."

"Nevertheless, you did handle that well."

"I didn't handle anything, Molly. He is not so terrible." While she was not necessarily any more partial to Kinney than the usual producer, she did concede a soft spot for him by the end of the brunch. Maybe it was due to a newfound understanding of him. Much in the way you can always literally see the perceptions change in the eyes of the audience as an unsympathetic character is made compassionate merely by the gathering of a few secret details or select thoughts revealed. During the small talk, Kinney was quite charming, and almost entirely forthright about his ambition to make, keep, and protect his money. He was not filled by wild theories or the rich man's justifications, nor did he feel ashamed about his success and his drive to it. He had worked hard in the tobacco business, seen it peak and then watched it fall dangerously close to the point of shattering, which he said as a father and husband nearly scared him to death. If he were young and single he might not have cared—he had spent so much of his youth traipsing around Europe with a modest sum that seemed like a bounty—but when he looked into the fearless eyes of his children he knew that he would do anything in his power to keep them that way. In some respects, that's what Venice of America was, a mixing of the dreams of his youth with a capital venture. He told her he was not that complicated, and she thought he was right. But she did not find him to be a particularly simple character either. The mark of the successfully ambitious.

"Are you ready to go in now?" Max asked.

"You are the one who closed the door."

Sarah slipped in behind Max. They stood at the back of the hall. Below them the last remnants of 9, rue d'Antin's interior were being hauled off to the right, while stage left saw Alexandre directing his crew in preparation to raise the walls of the church of Sant'Andrea della Valle. The actors sat in pairs with their faces buried in tattered scripts reminding themselves of the lines. They had changed roles quickly before. Perhaps a bit unexpected, but not particularly surprising. And in spite of their initial reactions (which Max described as filled with sighs and eye rolling), they all had returned easily to the business at hand. They were of course professionals dedicated to the craft. They studied and worshipped it. And unlike Sarah, most were hungry with ambition to stay alive in the industry. They must have equally worshipped and despised her position. To have made it. To not have to audition and hope and pray that you are given parts. To not lay awake nights and think of the shitty jobs that you will have to do in order to keep acting. To not walk into rehearsals questioning your talents and wondering if today will be the last. Sarah must have been the living embodiment of every single dream that her company of actors shared. And to them, she would have simply answered that she worshipped their passion for theater—one that extended beyond business. Their pure love for the heartbreak of art.

"I am not ready now," she said to Max.

"Sarah, they are waiting for you. They want to start reviewing *La Tosca* for tomorrow."

"They don't need me right now."

"At least for a line run-through."

"Molly, please just take me back to my room. I am telling you that I cannot do this right now." She spoke in a forceful whisper. "I have neither the enthusiasm nor the energy that the company will require of me at this time. They are better off temporarily to go at it alone."

"Sarah . . ."

"Molly, please."

"Do you prefer your railcar or the hotel room?"

"Whichever is closest."

VINCE BAKER REALLY WANTED A CIGARETTE.
Back downtown, he walked to Pershing Square and rode the Angels Flight funicular railway up to Broadway, and north to Temple Street, where he briskly trekked over toward Olive.

Once on Olive, Baker stopped and looked upward at a towering edifice that he had strangely never noticed before, like the long silhouette that stretches to announce you, but you forget that it is there. The unfamiliar building loomed over him. Its two columns split by the steps to the entrance and capped in sultans' hats blocking out the pinkly fading sky. Stained glass windows whose colors were muted by gray were lost with the setting sun. By design it was a simple structure. Generous curvatures and delicacies touched by the sculptor's hand cast its elegance.

He was caught in the building's shadow, as though a trespasser under the watchful eye of a stingy neighbor. Baker felt the light begin to evaporate, leaving a strange misty illumination that erased any sense of time. This is how prisoners must feel. Stripped of time. Where days and nights invert, wrapped around each other until they become indistinguishable. You need something to ground you, like the smell of a flame burning paper, and the soothing smoke that fills your mouth after a long drag. He had interviewed a crook named Skip Nelson once in the bowels of the L.A. county jail. Nelson had been picked up on orders of Mayor McAleer. Nelson had been kind of a loudmouth, with a history of larceny and unproven assaults. He had screamed out threats at Mayor McAleer once at a rally and then a week later made some impure suggestions about the mayor's wife, thus making him property of the city of Los Angeles. The fact that Theodore Roosevelt was stumping through the basin only extended Nelson's stay. So while most of the reporters were joining Roosevelt, McAleer, and all the other dignitaries over California oyster cocktails, Montalvo potato croquettes, and filet of Arizona beef at the Westminster Hotel, Baker sat in a cell, trying to get Nelson to talk about anything other than being railroaded by a man who believed his authority superseded the Constitution of the United States. It was an interview that yielded nothing, except enough crazy ramblings to build the mayor's case. But what he remembered most was Nelson bumming a smoke off him when he first sat down; and Nelson's eyes had been dark and hollow like the fluid had been sucked from them. Deep rings below the sockets that were in the accelerated process of molding to the skull. But he lit that butt. Under the orange ember his eyes yielded some life. Nelson didn't say another word until he finished the cigarette. Then asked for another. His only connection to normalcy. One thing to keep him alive. Until he died of mysteriously natural causes alone in a cell, with no reason for a postmortem despite the holster in his head perfectly tailored for a billy club.

Baker shouldn't be such a pansy about it. He should walk down to Second, bum a smoke from the first passerby, and march right up to the cathedral, tell the bishop that he is ready to talk, and could Conaty kindly share that bottle of booze that he surely keeps hidden, probably a three-quarter-full bottle of Jack Daniel's, square and weighted by its black label, a fluted neck confident yet lonely. And beside it would be two shot glasses that looked unused for some time, but still were noticeably free of dust. "Help yourself. Please," the bishop would say. His charm would be so real it would feel disingenuous. "We have much to discuss." And they could sit there together, killing the bottle and wondering how one barely significant person could compromise their professional dignities. Then they could figure how to finally do her in, so that they could return to their respective higher callings.

And in the midst of the mutual confession, Baker would

never mention to Conaty about having written the letter at the hotel. Or at least not in the fashion that he did. He had come off sounding childish and impudent, driven by the strains of a jealous lover below the balcony. It made him embarrassed just to think about it. Baker had made this assignment personal in a way they he didn't fully understand—quickly the story that he didn't want became the object of his desires. He could have analyzed it with a simple psychology, that he craved all the things he could never touch, but the basic-ness of that was insulting. Instead what he needed to negotiate was in understanding what he cared most about. He had convinced himself all along that he was the maverick who had ridden out from the wildest of the west into Los Angeles to expose the high rollers who gambled away everybody's future in an effort to line their own pockets. That he was the badass around town who kept the place honest. But perhaps he had forgotten his own honesty. There are those rare times when the mirrored walls that you put around yourself to imprison and protect your self-image become chipped and worn. Then suddenly you are looking through glass. You see the whole world out in front of you. And it is large. Goddamn it is big. And it expands all around you, and the sky arches up as an infinite hood, and there are faces and bodies so much larger and more meaningful than yours running in circles just to get around you. In other words, you realize how small you are. Everybody has been there. Huntington. Johnson. Doheny. Conaty. They had all looked through that window at one point. The fuel for their desperation to be larger. The chase for immortality, where the larger the letters for their names on the building are, the larger their memories live on, ensuring that they will always dwarf guys like Baker for all eternity. And something had made them see it, their own personal bush burning that gave them the nasty vision. And at that point it is all a matter of what you do with it. You can inflate yourself larger than life. Or you can wilt. Or be like most, and do whatever you can do to curtain the window and convert it back to a mirror where you continue your life in the safety to which you are accustomed.

Baker stood under the shadow of the immense structure, unsure of what to do. His past few days had been spent in the presence of an imposter. One who gives the appearance of ordinariness through her slight build, her coy gestures and ingratiating manner. But in truth Sarah Bernhardt was, and always would be, casting a shadow across him. And the fact that he even thought he could touch the edge of her world now seemed ridiculous. His letter must have looked so stupid to her, or even worse—insignificant.

He knew that he was not going into the Cathedral of our Lady of Angels. He could never willingly support the bishop's agenda (nor could he imagine sharing a drink with Conaty in some illusion of camaraderie). And as much as he wanted to run back to the King George Hotel to intercept his letter, that scene too had been concluded. He knew he had to fold his hand. He had broken the reporter's key rule: He had let the minutiae betray the obvious.

Tomorrow morning he would walk right into Graham Scott's office and quit on the spot. He wouldn't bother to explain how his integrity had been punctured, and that this fact was proof enough that it was time to hang it up. He wouldn't bother to try to defend himself by saying that he needed to get out before he was assigned to the new roller skating ordinance for downtown sidewalks, or the potential early closure of banks on Saturday evenings. There was still real news in this town that had to be covered, he would tell Scott, and it would only kill him not to be part of it. For example, the fallout from last year's land bust in Redondo Beach still remained untouched. Or just the other day, the massive Santa Fe depot contract had been inked. A quarter of a mile of building to be constructed on Santa Fe Avenue, just blocks from where he stood. And every paper in town seemed to be okay with it; they ran their pieces as though the depot were one more monument to the magnificence of Los Angeles. And not one reporter or editor even wondered or questioned how the builder, Carl Leonardt, had been awarded the contract. Baker wouldn't be suggesting that Leonardt had done anything wrong, however it should still be looked into, right? But the new journalism conspiracy seemed to be to tout anything that made the town look better (while ignoring the underside), and then rely on the mundane scandals to replace the hard news. And you go where your editor sends you, those are the only stories that you need to grab. That's the job now. Baker would tell Scott that he would rather leave than be a restrained observer. He could only imagine the reaction. Scott would laugh and say that Baker just got his balls busted by a broad—what else is new?—but that's no reason to quit. It's part of being a newspaperman. And then Scott would fade into his antiquated edict about their duty to comfort the tormented, and torment the comfortable—the newsroom philosophy that only lived in the memories of men of Scott's generation. But the truth would always be cautiously unspoken, that this was now a business with corporate interests like anything else, and that if guys like Baker wanted to stay in it, then they were going to have to learn how to adapt. Scott would lean over paternally and tell him that he had to stop taking it so seriously, because taking things too seriously only leads to taking things too personally. Baker knew that in order to avoid Scott's lectures he was just going to have to quit with nothing other than a two- or three-sentence resignation speech. It would be his last act of dignity as a journalist.

The shadow stretched long and thin, holding him in place. He wasn't quite ready to go home yet (and cashing it in at Willie's also felt too predictable, with its usual drinks and slobbering pheromones—a painful confirmation of his real status). Instead Baker thought he would just sit there for a while. Maybe all night. Wait until the morning sun shone again and wiped away the shadow. Then he would head downtown to hand his career back to Scott. Throw his desk belongings into a shopping bag, then go to his Pico apartment and load up the still unpacked boxes onto the bed of a truck heading east, hitching a ride back to Phoenix. Perhaps he could herd ostriches on his Uncle Martin's farm, and then go join the ranks of defected journalists to write a book that told the firsthand plight of the common man. In between days he might get to know his family a little more. Brag about his L.A. days, dropping the names of those he had covered, sadly reminded of his frustrations when Sarah Bernhardt was who they undoubtedly would want to know about. He would tell them. Watch their faces turn dumb with awe. Maybe submit to the lies that all memories tell, and forget the humiliation; instead embellish her importance and his role in it. After being plagued by questions about her, Baker would excuse himself for the bathroom. There he would stand before the mirror. He'd stare deep into the reflection, looking to find the remnants of the man who hadn't been seduced and trapped by the promise of Los Angeles.

But before he went near his office or the Pico apartment, Baker knew he would have to make a slight detour. Stop off at the local offices of the Santa Fe Railway Company. Do a little digging. Drum up a cigarette. Ask a few questions. See what anybody there might have to say about Carl Leonardt.

THERE WAS NOTHING COMFORTING about the room at the King George. Although her clothes and books and papers were scattered around the room, it still felt every bit as impersonal as the hotel room that it was. Beneath the bed she spotted the edition of the *Herald* that had run the original story. Just a dog-eared corner teasing out, a subtle reminder of how public her private issues were. And she almost wanted to pull it out, a pinch to remember that she wasn't dreaming. But instead she walked closer and kicked it farther beneath the bed.

Max had said he would run down to the theater to inform the company of the delay. He would tell them to keep working, and that Madame would join them after a brief rest. After he left, she went into the bathroom and turned the faucet handles of the bath, swiping her hand beneath the stream to test its temperature. She turned it off and looked into the tub at the gentle ripples washing up against the side, banging anxiously until they eventually faded into the depth of the light blue water. She left her skirt on, but pushed the hem up past her knees, then sat herself on the edge of the tub and dangled her feet in the warm water, soaking her aching right leg. It took her back to Uncle Faure's farm again. Seven years old. By herself at his pond. The water has been heated from the sunlight, and it is only as she steps out deeper that she will find the sudden coolness of the undercurrent. And the fish swim around her feet, tickling at the toes, and sometimes pecking the heels, as though mistaking them for food. From a patch of grass that fits just into the curve of her spine, she can watch the clouds blow across the sky, cleansing the blue like a sponge, spotless and shiny. And this is where the seven-year-old Henriette-Rosine imagines the rest of her life. The wedding, the husband, the two children, the servant, the diamonds. And she imagines her name being spoken on every pair of lips in France, and wonders how difficult it will be to shop or dine amid all the adulation. But it will not be hard on her husband because he will also be known throughout France—probably a war hero—but pity the children who are the victims of their parents' success, until they find their own. Finally she narrows it down to being an actress—but a different kind of actress. She will be noble. A lady. And her mother will be proud (she would make sure to thank her during every interview), and Mama can even come to live with her and her family, and they will keep the spare room ready for Papa once he finally comes back from his travels in China. Under that deep blue sky, Henriette-Rosine reaches up to hug the world while kicking her feet against the water, as though the pond is ordained with a magical power.

Now all these years later she sat in a strange hotel, her tired trodden feet soaking in a porcelain tub of man-made warmth. Many of those plans that she dreamed by Uncle Faure's pond had come true—some distorted, and others entirely mangled, if not neglected. There was no way that she could have known at the age of seven that even in dreams there are choices to be made. Everything good comes at the sacrifice of something else. And she inhaled deeply, trying to taste the pure air of the Neuilly farm, but instead took in the trailing remnants of a fresh coat of hotel paint. She had made all those plans, but had stopped there. She could not remember any time after that summer at Uncle Faure's that she had opened her eyes and imagined something else. From the moment she had dreamed this future, ambition set in, and she went about in the most practical manners to make it come true. And now she sits, knowing that Max will soon burst through the washroom door, having calculated some way to muster enthusiasm for patron-brunch-number-one-million-and-four that will keep the dream floating along. But maybe fifty-five years later it is time to imagine something new, and then kick in the ambition to make that come true. Like really leaving acting. Just slide out of this Sarah Bernhardt skin and let Henriette-Rosine take over (but in a lucid and rational state, for once). She looked up at the ceiling and imagined it as a blue sky. She arched her back slightly and kicked her feet in the water. She saw it all as clear as a day at Uncle Faure's. Stepping from one dream into the next.

As predicted, Max did knock on the bathroom door, after letting himself into the hotel room. She kicked the bathwater, watching the small waves tide up against the checkered tile backsplash. Let him knock another time or two. Weary him. Until her news about leaving will be a relief.

His knock didn't lessen. He was worried about the schedule, he called out. She kicked at the water again. It was still warm. She was going to tell him. Poor Molly was about to get more than he ever could have imagined. But soon he would find that the anger and resentments were just a by-product of this lifestyle. He would thank her after he was done hating her. But hopefully he will see that it was her dream that brought Max Klein to life, and that it will be her new dream that continues to bring him life. He just needs to continue to trust.

She pulled her feet from the tub, delicately balancing while she reached for a towel. She was not going to rush. While she let the unused tub drain, Sarah rubbed the terry cloth over her left foot but forgot her right. She opened the door as he spoke her name, his voice sounding increasingly feminine. He didn't even notice Sarah standing in a partial puddle in the lavatory doorway, with her arms crossed over her ribs.

She let a moment pass before she spoke in a calmed voice. "Molly, I am right here."

"I just don't want to get behind schedule is all."

"Molly," she repeated. It took every bit of her willpower not to tell him that he should catalog his expression. The way that his eyes seem to physically harden, his jaw bone nearly breaking out the cheeks. These were the emotions that actors treasured. Complete moments when the body has taken over the mind. She walked over to the bed and collapsed on it, doubling over a pillow and wedging it under her neck. "Now come here." She patted the bed. "Come lay beside me."

Max sat down obligingly but did not lay back.

"Come on," she said, "lie back. Gaze at the stars with me. See if you can find me up there in the hemisphere." She reached over and wrapped her hand around his fingers, squeezing gently. "I think my Molly is still feeling hurt. Come lie down. You refused my invitation in the train. Will you refuse me again? I want to tell you something. Please let me tell you why."

She drew her knees up toward her chest and worked her feet under the bedspread, as though dipping them back into Uncle Faure's pond, ready to start committing herself to the dream. "It is time for me to leave." The word *leave* caught in her throat.

"Excuse me?"

"I cannot act anymore." And the sound of those words seemed to come from some other place in the room, distant from beyond her body. When she was onstage assuming her characters, they became a part of her. It was their hearts that pumped through her chest. Their nerves that rattled her spine. Their breaths that she tasted and inhaled. But once she had to speak passionately from her own being, Sarah felt no connection. As though she had sacrificed herself for all those characters.

Max did not quite respond with the emotive outburst that she had anticipated. Instead he lay flat on his back, his eyes traversing the ceiling. "Don't worry," he said. "I will smooth things out for you."

"You don't understand." Her voice still did not sound convincing. Instead it fell rather flat and indifferent. "I can't match their passion anymore. I am just a maypole for the young actors to dance around."

"Perhaps this has been partially my fault," Max said with hardly a pause. Now it was time for his prepared speech. "I probably have not considered the pressures that you have been under. For that I apologize. But we'll be done with the tour soon. By the time we go back to France this will seem like a lost dream. Back to normal. We'll be trying to remember what the bishop's name even was."

She shook her head, but all she could muster was a quiet no. "It is more than forgettable bishops." It was all building inside her, ripping apart her gut and pushing on her rib cage as though it might shatter and splinter into a thousand kindling shards. She felt the curse of the French woman, where emotion is a closed-door endeavor, and any display that is shown outwardly is likely to label you somewhere between whore and demented. Or a world-renowned actress. She had never felt more debilitatingly ordinary.

"Our last chance for a thorough run-through is at four today." He was already on with the schedule, and planning. "We can work out some bugs after dinner, in order that we're ready for the first curtain tomorrow. You have a little more time here if you need it. Rest up. Gather some strength. Then you can enter the glorious diva at four."

"I am not doing tomorrow night's show," she said. "Or any show again."

He turned his head to her, awkwardly twisting his back. "Darling, the hysterical hour is over. You've already used up your comfort time. So now we are down to business."

His matter-of-factness and ease with the situation suggested that she had made these types of declarations before—something that Max obviously attributed to jitters and pressures. And the way that he clapped his hands with such a rise-and-shine bravado and told her that the best cure at this point was a nice long bath, followed by a spoiling of Burgundy from the last case in his room, topped off by a good solid nap was further indication that all this was nothing more than routine. But this was not the regular accumulation of demands and threats and insolent posturing that accompanied her stubbornness. This decision was a conscious philosophical verdict born from soul searching and examination.

Max pushed up from the bed. "Now shall I run a proper bath for you?"

"No." She did not move from under the covers. "You are not listening. I quit . . . I quit being an actress forever."

Max's body swayed with the irritation of someone late for an appointment. "Explain to me."

"I can't." She sighed. "You will just think that it is everything that you have heard before."

"You never explain *why* you are going to quit. You tell me the same thing every time—that there is no way that you can explain it to me in a manner that I will take seriously."

"I have never . . . "

"As predictable as the full moon."

Sarah pulled the covers up over her head, drowning herself in her own breath. She closed her eyes to make the darkness even darker, trying to recall this patterned conversation that Max alluded to. Maybe she was like one of those idiots that you always hear about—they can't wipe their own asses but can play the piano with genius precision. Maybe it was faulty wiring that only allowed her to activate her feelings in performance. She kicked the covers off with a rage of emotion that felt more liberating than it did angry. "I am done," she said. "Retired."

Max walked into the bathroom, apparently ignoring her. He closed the door partway. The faucet squealed, and then the force of water burst into the bathtub.

"Molly, I will not be there today," she yelled.

The sound of water rushed even harder.

"Do you hear me? I will never step foot on a stage again. I will not be there at four today. I will not be there ever."

He called from the bathroom. "Should I put the bath salts in? Is it that kind of bath?"

"Do what you please," she said to herself and pulled the covers back up, tucking them in around her neck. Maybe she would try to tell him once more, but probably she would have to quit before it became a reality. He would have to be sitting there at the 4:00 P.M. rehearsal nervously tapping his feet. She could picture him looking at the rear door in a combination of fury and disappointment each time that it opened and she wasn't there. At some point Max would have to figure it out—reflect back on what she had been saying in the hotel room about losing the passion and the fight. He would have to give up his opium jag excuses and realize how serious she had been. And then she would be waiting for him here in the hotel room. She would still be under the covers, ready to comfort him. Hold him with the reassurance that what they were about to embark on would be fine.

Max stepped out of the bathroom and pointed to the door. "It is ready for you, dear."

Sarah didn't move. She didn't smile or nod.

"Oh, please," he said. "You are not mad at me for not taking you seriously. You know that I always do. It's just that we have lost so much time after the change in plays, so we need to eliminate one step from the routine. Let's just see this one through, get on to Paris, and then you can quit the theater business from there. But for now you should rest and relax in your bath, and then be at the stage at four." He looked too rushed to have a definable expression.

"Don't wait for me."

"Please. Save it for Paris."

Sarah pulled the blanket up over her face.

She left the covers over her head until she heard the door close. Even though she could barely breathe.

SHE HEARD MAX'S FOOTSTEPS fall away down the hall. But when they stopped, Sarah pulled the covers back over her head. The footsteps started again, thankfully fading in the distance, instead of returning for one more round of sparring. She stayed in bed. She wondered if her new life would afford her the comforts that she had become accustomed to. Maybe reduced to some level of charming squalor that eschewed the bourgeoisie yet had no true revolutionary or radical convictions—more a matter of gliding through and enjoying her life. Perhaps a quiet retirement, reinvesting herself in the occasional company of her son, Maurice (of course that is its own story altogether). She pictured her future in a modest fourth-floor walk-up apartment. She would be able to add some air of romance to the flat, instead of it being like a traditional actor's flophouse (although the presence of all her pets—Bizibouzou the parrot, Darwin the monkey, and all the dogs might suggest otherwise).

She would be all right.

People would probably still care what she had to say (even though she wouldn't care anymore). And at least this ongoing war with the Visigoths of morality might end, or at least see a truce that would fade from stagnation. And certainly all thoughts of opium would vanish (as they already did just thinking about it).

She had had a brilliant career. But, like the members of her company, the real passion had been reserved for her hungry youth. The days when the only serious matters were the moments between the opening curtain and the final bow. When she awoke each morning with gloved fists ready to take on the world, swinging and flailing, but always with a puckish smile. Nobody worried about anything. If she ran into trouble she would just make something up to cause it to go away. She had always been the master of weaving her own reality. She knew that. Most of the people around her thought she was impossible. That she was unable to see the truth in the world around her. She would take adversity and pretend it never happened. She would make up stories to explain away the bad past. She knew they whispered that she would have to open her eyes one day, that life is not an ongoing production with her as its director. And many in her circle treated her as though she were delusional, unable to distinguish between the stage and reality. But wasn't that right where she wanted them? Keeping them off balance. Never being able to fully read her, and always relying on her to navigate the latest reality. In truth it was power. The unstable are always the most powerful. Unpredictability is a dangerous weapon. And even more so when it is being handled by puppet strings with a nod and a wink. She had used it to rule over everyone—her crew, the newspapers, the promoters. And the audiences loved her for it. Everywhere she went in the world, they gathered around her and waited for her to do *something*.

But somewhere along the line the act became routine, and she stopped fully trusting herself and her motive. She questioned her own versions of events. Her attempts at unpredictability seemed contrived and rehearsed. She had started to lose control. And once she lost the ability to control, the outside events that she was trying to deflect began to creep in and overwhelm her. Break her down. And those imbeciles around her who had whispered behind her back would never have once considered that she had only been protecting them. Instead they stripped her of her battle armor and sent her to the Coliseum to face the black-veiled gladiators, still leaving her there today. Even out on that pier, reaching into her arsenal for one last single shot, her interior demons had overwhelmed her capability to ward off the conservative reactionaries. The stunt on the pier may have brought on a wave of nostalgia for some (*we have our old Sarah back*), but in truth it did nothing other than to reinforce her helplessness. Nothing went away. It just seemed to get worse. Hence the need to escape, medicinally and literally.

Sarah cinched the covers around her neck. She couldn't shake the chill that vibrated her bones.

The hands on the clock faced her at 3:11 P.M., leaning to the right with arms outstretched for an awkward embrace. She wanted to yank the covers over her head and not come out until it was after 4:00 P.M., with the rehearsal well under way without her. And there would be Max, nervously twitching, ready to ingest himself until he could disappear and leave nothing but a small spot of saliva where he had just stood. Kinney's fury would rage though the theater while the actors paced not too far from their blocking marks, wondering if indeed the show does go on. Maybe a reporter would be there calmly taking notes, never moving from his seat, bowing his pen like Nero while the whole theater burned down. And his story would run the next day, and the bishop would tack it up on the announcements board in the cathedral where it would take on a shrine quality, a memorial to victory and perseverance—the trophy for decency. And then the bishop will go on and fight the next battle, realizing somewhere down the line how little effect executing Sarah Bernhardt had on the wages of morality.

She looked up at the clock once more. That minute hand wouldn't move if she hit it with a chisel.

She rubbed her feet together to warm them. The bones and calluses only added to the discomfort.

She really had no problem with her career ending. She just couldn't stand to see it end this way. The more she pictured her absence in the theater, the more she felt a certain cowardice. Maybe that is how Henriette-Rosine would exit, by never taking the stage at all, but Sarah Bernhardt commanded the boards. The theater only came to life when she entered it, and when she exited she sucked out the life in a trailing tornado's tail. She should be giving a farewell speech to her company, for all the times they had stood behind her. She owed it them, especially to Constant and Edouard. A dramatic recitation that rivaled the best of Shakespeare, and then leave with the footlights in her fists, keeping the power and the victory for herself.

But getting out of bed felt impossible.

She expected Max would knock one more time. He didn't believe her. He never believed her dramatics. He was the one who usually saw through her. That was what made him such a good manager. Only this time he should be seeing her seriousness. Not trying to convince her with some imbecilic speech that this is some kind of pattern. That kind of insulting talk suggested that her fits and starts were unruly, and that perhaps there was some delusion about her realities. She should have told him that it must have been a true miracle that she became the most successful woman in the whole world. A real miracle. Maybe that would buy her a seat in Bishop Conaty's house.

She slid off the bed and went into the bathroom. If she submerged her body into the pool, the water would initially burn the skin surface in an almost sensual manner, a thin clear line singeing its way over her stomach and breasts before it settled at her neck. And the heat would relax her muscles, slowing down her heartbeat and draining out a final restless breath until she felt completely relaxed in wombed comfort.

Sarah turned around with force, almost falling into the tub headfirst (and wouldn't that make a headline ending). She was not going to get in the bath. Not going to give Max the satisfaction of honoring his routine.

Nor would she ever drain the bath.

She went back to her bed, pulling the covers up, while the edges burned across her stomach and breasts, before settling comfortably at her neck.

The light was growing dim. It could get cold so quickly once the sun considered sinking. And she wished it were tomorrow already. By then there would only be bruises. The blows long ago forgotten and turned to myth.

WITH WHAT SHE EXPECTED was Max's knock, Sarah opened the door to see instead the desk clerk. "Pardon me, Madame," he said. "But I have a message I have been asked to personally deliver." He handed it to her and stood there as she read it, as was customary in case a reply was warranted (although the reporter had clearly instructed him not to bother). Her face bent into a smile, and tiny fragments of lines burst around her eyes, showing an age that Dolph had not noticed in her before.

She glanced up at him, his skin-and-bones frame willing itself not to twitch from nerves. "This Monsieur Baker is a young man, I would guess. He does not yet know the difference between thinking things and sharing them."

Dolph shrugged.

"Another ruffian. A bad boy iconoclast. The world produces a new one every five minutes. And that's the irony now, isn't

it? They're spitting out duplicates as fast as it takes to walk out
the door and to the pier. The real bad boys are the ones who
do everything by the book. Clean-cut and in bed by eight. They
take an occasional drink at the proper social moment, with
barely a fantasy about bending a lady over with a slapping
hand held above their heads. They read one or two books a
year, nothing controversial, nothing too thought provoking,
and then they blush at the suggestion of any risqué parts.
Those are the real bad boys. They are the ones who truly face
the world alone."

Dolph moved his heels a little closer together. Adopting a
more formal posture, as Mr. Kinney had instructed all his staff.
"Do you have a reply, Madame?"

Sarah paused, then drew in a long inhalation. Finally she
let it go with an outstretched arm. "Yes," she said, returning
the paper. "Please take the letter back and hold it at the desk.
Perhaps he will realize his foolishness, and we can give him
the option of retrieving the letter and disposing of it as quickly
as he can."

Dolph bent the message into an uncommitted fold. He
nodded and backed away to leave.

"Pardon," she said. "I am sorry but I do not have any money
to offer for your services. I will see that Monsieur Klein takes
care of that. And what is your name?"

"Dolph."

"Dolph," she repeated. "I wonder if I know your parents.
Dolph. Perhaps I have seen your parents marching through the
streets of Paris and shooting little babies. Or maybe those were
your father's bullets lodged into the bodies of all those boys
who were laid up in my hospital during the war. It is indeed a
small world, isn't it, Dolph?"

"Perhaps I should just leave you to your room now."

"Perhaps," she said. "Off with you. And don't forget to tell your father hello for me. Tell him that Sarah Bernhardt remembers every bullet that shed the skin of every French boy. Now off." Then she leaned her head through the door frame and yelled down the hallway to Dolph, "There really is no need to worry. Monsieur Klein will see that your efforts are well compensated."

3:45 P.M. THE CLOCK ACTUALLY HAD MOVED. She was waiting for Max. She had gone to the closet and buttoned up a white chemisette slightly into perfection, the cambric veiling her cleavage and framing her neck. Then she slipped on a white waist shirt, slowly buttoning it to bring the pirate flounces into form. She stepped into her black peau de soie skirt, the plain tailored silk falling naturally against her form. She didn't bother to look in the mirror. She was dressed to go to her own funeral. She pushed her hair up, bringing life to her pillow-flattened mane.

"My lord, you look sensational." Max looked relieved upon arrival, as if he had expected to find her buried deep in her bed, black rings circling her eyes, and a weak and frail voice fully dehydrated of spirit. "Let's find your boots, and I will help you lace them up," he offered hopefully.

She decided not to fight. Not to toy or tease.

"Sit down beside me," she said, patting the bed. "Please, before we go."

He looked at her with his head cocked. His suspicion was getting the better of him.

"You should always trust me."

Max dug his hands into his pockets, they bulged and crawled as he scratched his thighs. He nodded. Bit his lip. Looked ridiculously young, as though the situation had drawn him back into the awkwardness of a closeted sixteen-year-old boy, tiptoeing across each day, waiting for the wrath of his father's disappointment, and the violent form it was likely to take. It was ironic that she had become a father figure to him. Wasn't that one of the things that these puritans hated her for—how she had sometimes played the opposite gender on the stage? (And it often was Hamlet for God's sake, not some depraved hermaphroditic child molester.) Her naysayers should take hold of this one—acting as a father to a queer man. That would almost certainly give them license to kill.

After shuffling his feet and kicking at the floor, Max finally sat down. His weight barely dented the bed.

Sarah took his hand. "I just want you to know that I love you. You will always be my Molly. In the words of Marguerite: *When you saw me spitting blood you took my hand.*" And she meant it. She may have despised the way that he puppy-trailed the ass scents of the Kinneys of the world, appearing to straddle the lines of allegiance in some form of arrogant collusion, but still the truth of it was that when the band stopped playing and the last drinks had been served, he came home with her. Night after night.

Max squeezed her hand. It was sweaty. He didn't say anything. She knew he was terrified that his words would only come out sounding maudlin.

"Things have to be different is all." It was only when the words left her mouth and vanished into the room that she truly understood the impossibility of the statement.

Max bit down on his bottom lip. "You should just come

to the rehearsal. Once you're there . . ." He was starting to lecture. He stopped himself. "You should just come."

And she thought to say something about the old days. About how they would never have moved another inch without a blast of cocaine or a smoke of opium. And the feeling was nostalgic without the brilliance of sentimentality, a statement only designed for sharing a laugh or common connection. But Max, in his vigilant patrol state, would take that as a sign of weakness. Being lured by a temptress. And he would say it as such, leaving her to feel mortally stupid and pathetically old. Instead she just nodded, and said, "I know. I am planning to come to the theater."

"It is only a few minutes from now."

She flamboyantly threw her arms around his neck, roping him in closer to her until she held his cheek an inch from her mouth. She smacked her lips in a kiss that deliberately fell short. "Molly, I know that you care for me. Enough so that I can forgive you treating a sixty-one-year-old woman as though she is a wide-eyed girl. But leaving the theater is something that I am going to do." She then leaned in the extra inch, feeling her spine extend, and touched her lips to his properly smoothed cheek. "Let's go," she whispered. "I plan to tell the company myself."

"I'm only looking out—"

"Love me and you'll trust me." She kissed his cheek again, and then released him from her hold.

He turned his back slightly. Not out of shame or irritation, but more in the manner of one who finds himself helplessly helpless. When the power is tripped, and the words that would usually come to mind just seem to form sounds that predate language. His toe ground into the floor, smothering out the last ember of righteousness, and she knew that if he did turn his head around, that she would see his eyes filled by tears. He never liked to disappoint. Even the slightest suggestion sent him back into his shame. Bishop Conaty ought to get hold of him.

SARAH ASKED TO WALK the long route. She wanted some fresh air. Stretch her legs. Feel the freedom of the setting sun. She wanted to clear her head. Stroll by the canals. Ingest the ocean salts. They walked until they came to the edge of Venice Canal, where they stopped and looked across at Abbot Kinney's estate. For a moment it was almost tranquil. As though they could have been the sole occupants of this magnificent planet. They might have resigned themselves to an infinite monastic silence if she had not spoken in a sudden voice: "It is okay. You may stare if you like."

Max asked what she said.

"Him." She pointed over to the thin shadow from an adolescent tree.

He was a young man, perhaps still a boy. Nothing remarkable in stature. He looked afraid. He pulled at his fingers. "I'm sorry," he said. "I don't mean to stare." He held a notebook and a pen, trembling in the presence of the woman he had waited for, just for an autograph.

"Is it that you have never been in the presence of a star, or that you have never been in the presence of a French woman?" she said to the boy, ignoring Max elbowing her side.

The boy kicked his feet a little. He ran his hands along his chin, one that would not be bristled by a sloppy shave for a few more years to come. "I'm not sure I know how to answer that."

"Pardon?" She leaned forward. "You will have to speak louder."

"I said, I'm not quite sure how to answer that."

"Well, how about either, or."

Max tried to intercede by stepping forward to reach for the boy's book and pen. He tried to place his body between the two of them, hoping to ward her off. Perfectly timed she blocked Max, maintaining her place at the center stage marker.

"Look at him twisted into a knot," she said to Max. "His free hands are feeling up his arms each time I make eye contact with him. Like a misfit who wandered onto the stage and just noticed the audience through the footlights."

"I only request . . . ," he sputtered.

"Is it the mystique of the French woman that is throwing you? You no doubt have heard all the legends of the passion and seduction. And the way they can toy with a man. Or maybe it's our sophistication. That is always a threat to an American. But it makes you nervous. Right? Nervous. A woman who is your mother's age awakening you. Is that right, Monsieur Oedipus? You are afraid of the legend of the French seductress?"

The unfortunate boy could not look away from her. "I just wanted an autograph was all."

"A signature? Or is it the thought swirling through your head that you might be able to have this actress if you don't make any mistakes. This actress who is your mother's age— although you can't say that you really think that I look it. Nor would you admit to yourself, either." She pushed herself upright and shook her hair out. Smiled. Pleased with this scene. She then ripped the book from the boy's hand and stretched her name along the length of the page. "My name," she said to him. "And a story to go with it."

She turned around and took Max by the arm, pulling him to walk away. "Pardon me for not issuing a formal good-bye," she said, turning around. "But I am due at the theater any moment to bid a heartbreaking farewell to ones who love me even more than you."

The boy scampered off quickly, running as if guard dogs nipped at his heels, yet staring at the page the whole way.

Max just shook his head and said, "Sarah, you really shouldn't have."

"I know, Molly. I just wanted to be Sarah Bernhardt one last time."

They paused for a few minutes, staring over at Coral Canal. They didn't talk. Eventually they turned to make the processional march to the theater.

"I swear I smell steak searing," Sarah spoke. "I must be hungry."

"Maybe the little café at the end of Rose Street."

"Listen to you reciting the street names like a local."

"After the last few days I'm starting to feel like I was born here. And that I will die here."

"Oh, Molly."

Sarah closed her eyes. Inhaling the fantasy fragrance of red wine, pure chocolate, and savory meats. Imagining they were back in Paris and dreaming of possibilities. She rolled her shoulders forward in pleasure. "I swear," she cooed, "if you were not such a Molly I could really fall in love with you."

A STRANGE ANTICIPATION welcomed Sarah Bernhardt as she walked into the theater. The cast stood idly, scattered about the stage. Constant Coguelin and Edouard de Max were deep in thought, trying to recall their characters and hoping they hadn't been left behind in Salt Lake City or some other stop along the way. Irma Perrot, Marguerite Moreno, and Sacha Guitry formed a triangle, walking a circle in metered breaths while training their eyes on the person directly across from them. Standing in the darkened back at stage right, Ibé was guarding his wigs like a devastated parent, cracking his finger like a whip at anybody who dared approach him without invitation or permission. The technical crew all scattered about, tying off knots, testing footlights, ensuring the spot would work with the calcium carbonate gathered from Pasadena. And to outsiders like Kinney, it must have looked frantic. Disorganized bumbling fools crossing paths, unknowingly holding ends of the same rope and pulling in desperate frustration. But to Sarah, who stood a pace behind her longtime confidant, the evening sea air still following her through the shutting door, this looked as magnificent as the play itself. Stripped away of all the *conneries* and redundant exercises that Molly insists on for three days prior, and just leaving this night-before energy. Each crew member was so perfectly placed, doing exactly what he or she needed to be doing, flowing in and out of one another with the precision of ants stocking their kingdom. And in this one moment, this single solitary moment, she was glad that she had not quit from afar. Max looked back at her and nodded with a gingerly proud smile on his face. As though he had known that all he had to do was get her in the door, and all would return to normal. Maybe he had been right.

She stopped while Max kept walking. Nobody had noticed her yet. She held her hands flat against each other in prayer position, and drew her index fingers up to her mouth, resting the tips against her upper lip. She was truly going to make that announcement. Change the course of this whole drama. A play that had had a run longer than God knows when. And everybody drums up the same enthusiasm and emotion nightly, hearing cheers and applauding, but in the backs of their minds and the fronts of their hearts there is a nagging misery that they choose to ignore and then override it with rationales, forever fearful of breaking such a long string of success. But she was going to change the whole direction of this play of her life by rewriting one single scene. One simple scene toward the end of the final act (after all she was sixty-one now, and there should be no denying the realties of age), and she would breathe a new life into this drama that would inspire all to stop going through the motions, but instead start living.

Max stopped a full three paces ahead. "Come on, Sarah," he barked with a stage whisper. "Come watch their eyes light when they see you."

It was probably only one or two pairs of hands clapping. Then like an approaching train the volume increased, rolling across the stage. Even Ibé put down his wigs for a moment (spiking a comb through a long falling curl) and put his arms out with a walruslike clapping motion. And they were all standing, rising to their feet to see her—her own crew. It was the moment between the kiss and the sex. When he tells you that you are the most beautifully magnificent creature that he has ever laid eyes on—seducing you into believing his own myth.

Kinney himself was standing, breaking a commanding and paternal applause. Max stood beside him, his hands barely touching, avoiding eye contact with her. Maybe he was embarrassed to be found so quickly beside the Baron of Venice. Or perhaps it was his routine expression, the same predictable one that is known to accompany habitual lovers the morning after. She tried smiling at him with her dignified public smile, the same one worn by regals that gently stretches across the face like a fine line between invulnerability and the illusion of accessibility. She never could control expressions when they came from someplace real. She gave a subtle wink to let him know that Henriette-Rosine was hiding happily behind the curtain and waiting for him.

The crew stood side by side in front of the stage, forming a tunnel that led up to the edge. And she walked as far as she could, trying to keep up the eye contact with Max, trying to let him know that all would be okay; instead catching Kinney's proud and demanding eyes, as though his browbeaten daughter had finally captured the prince's heart.

Max stayed behind with the impresario while Constant's and Edouard's hands guided Sarah up to the stage and into the church of Sant'Andrea della Valle, where Cesare Angelotti was about to meet the painter Mario Cavaradossi, and thus begin the tragic fall of the strong but vulnerable opera star named Tosca.

Framed by Cavaradossi's mural in progress and Angelotti's youthful ambitions, both of which would soon witness their demises, Sarah drew in a deep breath. And in that breath the tragic will of Tosca entered her lungs and refreshed her blood cells until she was neither Henriette-Rosine nor Sarah Bernhardt. Instead, somewhere in between. Just where she needed to be.

EPILOGUE
March 29, 1920

Théâtre Sarah Bernhardt, Paris, France

THEY ask her to sign playbills. And she watches them recoil into the awkwardness of newborns trying to touch the world. Patrons of the arts. The powerful. The elite. Shrinking into helplessness in her presence. But in the midst of this lazzo scene, Max Klein appears in the center of the room, spotlighted after Sarah gives the stage to him. He clears his throat and announces in a confident manner that this reception area must be cleared. The houselights have dimmed and everybody needs to find their seats or else risk missing the opening curtain. He encourages them to enjoy the evening's performance, and reminds them Madame looks forward to meeting with them at the reception following the final curtain. They file out anxiously, fearful of missing the first act. And in that moment of silence when the last has left the room with the final breath of pageantry, it is just she and Max. And they don't share a word. Barely acknowledge the other's presence. After a passing of time Max looks up at her and speaks with a formality unique to the moment before she is set to take the stage. "Madame Bernhardt," he says as though the appointed minion to a head of state. "It is time to take your position."

SHE RUNS HER TONGUE over lips. Moistening them. The apron feels heavy. Black velvet curtains. She strokes them, watching the slow ripples that travel to the top. She is seventy-six years old now. She has lost her right leg to amputation five years ago, the result of a car accident (in Venice of all places), followed by a stage fall, and the subsequent gangrene. She sits in the chair that will be hers when she takes the stage. She rubs the stump from where her leg once fell. She swears that she feels her toes tickle. Strange, especially given that the opium has not been in her system since May of 1906. She is just out of view of even the most vigilant audience member. There is always one who is trying to look backstage. Trying to catch a glimpse in the wings. Waiting for recognition. A nod. A wink. Even a raised eyebrow. Imbeciles. One illusion is not enough for them. The last ripple finally reaches the top. Barely. Ridiculously slow. The curtain looks settled. She waits. Slowly sliding out of herself. Somehow she will slip into the character of Marguerite Gautier. It is kind of like dying. Where the life you know slides from your body, revealing each moment to you like a photograph in an album. An illusion of shadow and light, still and forgotten. From a distance it is nothing more than abstract images, imbued with relevance by the spaces you fill in. She sees the faces of all those hopeful girls who will never succeed. They flood her mind. Nervously standing backstage. Pushing sweaty hands against their dresses, waiting for the director's permission to display their wares, those five minutes that can destroy years of dreams. And something so simple seems so complicated. It's just art. It is just doing what you need to do, expressing things the only way you know how. But suddenly the artistic life becomes business. And every line that you learn has an impact on whether you will ever have the opportunity to speak the next one. And yes, sure, she could have said to hell with it, and paraded her talents down to some back alley theater and spoke the lines from a blacked-out room in a converted basement. She might even have had the same passion. Maybe more. But that is a possibility that she knows will never be answered. She never stood side by side with those hopeful girls. She was too busy being blinded by the footlights becoming who she is. The odd thing is that she never sees herself. Well, not quite true. Occasionally she sees images of Sarah Bernhardt, but they are no more she than they are Marguerite Gautier, Mrs. Clarkson, Jeanne d'Arc, or even Ethel Barrymore. Maybe that is what makes it so much easier to slip into character. She is forever naked.

MAX KLEIN WALKS UP TO HER. He shows her a note, and then pushes it deep into his pocket, the last swirl of curved ink disappearing. She can see him crumple it in his pants, the fabric bunching and wrinkling, gloved around his fist. "A message from President Millerand," he whispers, and she says, "Yes? Has he rewritten the play?" and Max replies softly, "No, just the usual good luck note." They both stand quietly. The murmur of the audience droning before them. Thousands and thousands of words that have blended into one indistinguishable sound

that is void of meaning. She turns to look at Max and steals a
full glance without his noticing. He is beautiful. Soft and tender
despite his tightly threaded expression and recent aging. He is
strength woven by a lifetime of insecurities. His devotion to
her is uncompromising, but she does not see him as subordinate
or lacking. It is the love of the spiritually connected. Lifetimes
of incarnations that have not-so-accidentally rounded the
corner into one another and partnered for yet another go-
around. It doesn't warm her like she thinks it should. Instead
it grounds her. Makes her place on the earth seem more
assured. A gravitational hand to hold in order to keep from
shooting off into outer space. She thinks to tell him that she
loves him. Not in the usual manners—the petulant child who
tosses out *I love you* as some form or apology or distraction,
nor as the invertebrate lacking in lucidity who suddenly finds
herself in love with the whole world. This would be real. The
kind that makes the skin crawl. But she decides against it. Too
unprofessional. She needs to be summoning Marguerite. Calling
on her to inhabit this body. Charging her with the energy being
conducted through the house. She is supposed to be driving out
Sarah Bernhardt. Freeing her for the next three hours until
she is harkened back for the final curtain calls. To love Max too
much is to endanger the moment. He looks back at her, evidently
not noticing her stare. In perfect synchronization he nods as
the houselights dim. She smiles at his perfection. It is her last
chance to say how much she loves him. She starts to round her
lips to form *I*, but instead pushes out a hard steady plosive that
contrasts with the pastoral breathiness of the single-vowel word
that speaks a thousand philosophies. She looks at him again.
This time she speaks: "Onward." The word hangs clear and
distinct, its edges sharpened and crisp among the blurred crowd

din. With her hands pressed against her stomach and feeling for breath, she prepares to take the stage. She has no choice.

SHE IS AT HOME.

IT'S LIKE AN ILLUSION, the way she paces the floor. Left with only one leg, her feet still seem to fall heavy, stomping the boards. Sometimes rattling the stage walls. She is solid. Rooted to the floor. And it extends beyond gravity. It is more a matter of connection. It is like language. She is the meaning created by the listener and the speaker. It is command. And yet, almost conversely, she seems to float across the stage. Gliding. As though all movement suffers no effort. Gliding among the actors as though they are inanimate objects and she is the breeze. *Strike that.* She is nothing like language. She is not a voice or a tool or an instrument to convey thought through the artifice of metaphor. She is meaning. In all its literal glory.

SHE DOESN'T EVEN FEEL herself breathe.

THREE HOURS LATER she is still onstage, seated on a stuffed feather bed that is draped by a thin comforter and bordered by a mound of pillows. She is costumed in a long white negligee with an embroidered lining that hangs below the neckline. Her face is powdered a consumptive white, and heavy black eyeliner helps to draw out the sickness. Her left leg hangs over the bed, the foot dressed in a lace slipper. The stump of her right is carefully hidden below the covers. Since the amputation her set designers have worked miracles to create the illusion that hides the phantom leg. She is about to die as Marguerite Gautier once again. Soon the character of Julie Duprat will enter and light two candles. She will kneel before the bed and watch the tragic figure scream out in pain with three long howls. There will be pauses, one beat longer than normal between each scream, and the theater will be in resolute silence, until the next howl picks up as the other fades away. And then she will sit up twice. Each movement is so simple and shapeless on its own, but within context she will be in desperation, reaching out with one final attempt to grasp onto her mortal life. Then she will cry out for Armand. She will scream for him as though he is just outside the theater on the Place du Châtelet, so close but unable to hear his own name. And the audience will all tense and sway their bodies, as though trying to help give her call more force, as though there truly is an Armand Duval standing right outside the stage doors on the boulevard. And tears will fill her eyes. They will crawl down her cheeks, running traces through the foundation. The theater will be stunned into silence, cooperative by their own tears. And then she will cough one time, enough blood will rise to stain her gown. And then she will die. She will not grasp for the floorboards as she used to. Partly because the loss of her leg has stilted her range of motion. Mostly though, she has come to see Marguerite's death less and less as a struggling battle to hang on to life, but instead as a willingness to let go in a slow silent mourning for her lost love and passion.

Divine Sarah is loosely based on real circumstance (and
draws from certain incidents and legends in Sarah Bernhardt's
life), but the drama, narrative, and most of the characters are
imagined. Combinations of characters have been formed into
one, and real circumstances have been bent and mutated for the
purposes of storytelling. Advance apologies to those protectors
of Sarah. But I think that she would have recognized the intent
behind this book—to create a truth that might have been hers
within a mostly fictitious world and setting.

I am indebted to Sarah's memoir *Ma Double Vie*, translated
by Victoria Tietze Larson, *La Dame aux Camélias* by Alexander
Dumas *fils*, the technical assistance of Bill Ratner, Alec Hodgins
and his French class, and the volumes of information in
public libraries and posted on various Web sites. And lastly
to the power of imagination that can take scatterings of facts

and fictions and create brand-new worlds. Something Sarah Bernhardt would believe in and support.

Special thanks to the people at William Morrow: Henry Ferris, for leading the charge; Michael Morrison, for his faith; and Lisa Gallagher and Sharyn Rosenblum, for their savvy.

Thanks to Nat Sobel. I am forever reminded that my words might be tucked away in a manila envelope in a drawer if not for him.

As always, thanks to Chuck Newman, Mel Saferstein, and Jerry Williams for being willing to help in a thousand different ways.

And finally, the love and support of friends and family.